AFFINITIES
AND OTHER STORIES

MARY ROBERTS RINEHART

THE WORKS OF
MARY ROBERTS RINEHART

AFFINITIES

THE REVIEW OF REVIEWS COMPANY
Publishers   NEW YORK
PUBLISHED BY ARRANGEMENT WITH GEORGE H. DORAN COMPANY.

CONTENTS

AFFINITIES

AFFINITIES
AND OTHER STORIES

AFFINITIES

I

SOMEBODY ought to know the truth about the Devil's Island affair and I am going to tell it. The truth is generally either better or worse than the stories that get about. In this case it is somewhat better, though I am not proud of it.

It started with a discussion about married women having men friends. I said I thought it was a positive duty—it kept them up to the mark with their clothes and gave a sort of snap to things, without doing any harm. There were six of us on the terrace at the Country Club at the time and we all felt the same way—that it was fun to have somebody that everybody expected to put by one at dinners, and to sit out dances with and like the way one did one's hair, and to say nice things.

"And to slip out on the links for a moonlight chat with you," said Annette, who is rather given to those little pastimes, the most harmless in the world.

We were all awfully bored that Sunday afternoon. Most of the men were golfing; and when you meet the same people all the time—day after day, dinner after dinner, dance after dance—anything new is welcome. Really the only variety we had was a new drink now and then. Some one would come home from his vacation with a brand-new idea in beverages and order one all round, and it was a real sensation.

That was all we had had all summer for excitement, except the time Willie Anderson kissed Sybilla—she was his wife—on a wager. They had been rather cool to each other for a month or so.

We would sit on the terrace and the conversation would be about like this:

"There's the Jacksons' car."

"Why on earth does Ida Jackson wear green?"

"Hello, Ida! When d'you get back?"

"Yesterday. Bully time!"

Just in time to save us from utter boredom somebody would yawn and remark:

"Here comes the Henderson car."

"Jane Henderson's put on weight. She's as big as a house! Hello, Jane!"

"Hello, everybody! My goodness! Why did I come back? Isn't it hot?"

More excitement for a minute and then more yawns. It was Ferd Jackson who suggested the affinity party. He had heard about what I had said on the terrace, and he came to me while Day was playing on the links. Day is my husband.

"Had a nice afternoon?" he asked.

"Only fair. Day's been underfoot most of the time. Why?"

"How'd you like a picnic?"

"I would not!" I said decisively. "I hate cold food and motoring in a procession until you choke with dust—and Day getting jealous and disagreeable and wanting to get home early."

"Poor little girl!" said Ferd, and patted my hand in a friendly way.

Ferd was a good scout always; we got along together pretty well and sat together at dinners whenever we could. He never made love to me or anything like that, but he understood me thoroughly, which Day never took the trouble to do. It is absurd, now that it's all over, to have the others saying he was my affinity or anything of the sort. I never cared for him.

"I didn't mean the usual sort of picnic," Ferd said. "How has it got its pretty hair fixed to-day? Rather nice, lady-love; but why do you hide your pretty ears?"

Lady-love was only a nickname.

"So I won't be able to hear Day bragging about his golf score. What sort of a picnic?"

"It's a peach of an idea!" Ferd said. "It came to me out of a clear sky. Every picnic we've ever had has been a failure—because why? Because they were husband-and-wife picnics. There's no trouble about a picnic where nobody's married, is there?"

"Humph! What's the peach of an idea? To get divorces?"

"Certainly not! Have husbands and wives— only somebody else's husband or somebody else's wife. You and I—do you see?—and Annette and Tom; Jane Henderson and Emerson Riley; Catherine Fredericks and that fellow who's visiting the Moores. How about it?"

"Day would have a convulsion, Ferd."

"Good gracious, Fanny!" he said. "Haven't you any imagination? What has Day got to do with it? You wouldn't tell him, of course!"

Well, that was different. I was rather scared when I got to thinking of it, but it sounded amusing and different. One way and another I see such a lot of Day. He's always around unless there's a golf tournament somewhere else.

"It's moonlight," Ferd said. "The only thing, of course, is to get off. I can stay over at the club or go on a motor trip. It's easy enough for the fellows; but the girls will have to work out something."

So we sat and thought. Day came in from the links just then and stopped by my chair.

"Great afternoon!" he said, mopping his face. "Y'ought to hear what I did to Robson, Fan—I drove off my watch and never touched it. Then he tried it with his. Couldn't even find the case!"

"Go away, Day," I said. "I'm thinking."

"Ferd doesn't seem to interfere with your thinking."

"He's negative and doesn't count," I explained. "You're positive."

That put him in a good humour again and he went off for a shower. I turned to Ferd.

"I believe I've got it," I said—"I'll have a fight with Day the morning of the picnic and I'll not be there when he gets home. I've done it before. Then, when I do go home, he'll be so glad to see me he'll not ask any questions. He'll think I've been off sulking."

"Good girl!" said Ferd.

"Only you must get home by ten o'clock—that's positive. By eleven he'd be telephoning the police."

"Sure I will! We'll all have to get home at reasonable hours."

"And—I'm a wretch, Ferd. He's so fond of me!"

"That's no particular virtue in him. I'm fond of you—and that's mild, Fan; but what's a virtue in Day is a weakness in me, I dare say."

"It's an indiscretion," I said, and got up. Enough is a sufficiency, as somebody said one day, and I did not allow even Ferd to go too far.

Annette and Jane and Catherine were all crazy about it. Annette was the luckiest, because Charles was going for a fishing trip, and her time was her own. And Ferd's idea turned out to be perfectly bully when the eight of us got together that evening and talked it over while the husbands were shooting crap in the grill room.

"There's an island up the river," he explained, "where the men from our mill have been camping; and, though the tents are down, they built a wooden pavilion at the edge of the water for a dining hall—and, of course, that's still there. We can leave town at, say, four o'clock and motor up there—you and Tom, Annette and——"

"I've been thinking it over, Ferd," I put in, "and I won't motor. If the car goes into a ditch or turns over you always get in the papers and there's talk. Isn't there a street car?"

"There's a street car; but, for heaven's sake, Fanny——"

"Street car it is," I said with decision. "With a street car we'll know we're going to get back to town. It won't be sitting on its tail lamp in a gully; and we won't be hiding the license plates under a stone and walking home, either."

There was a lot of demur and at first Annette said she wouldn't go that way; but she came round at last.

"I'll send a basket up late in the afternoon," Ferd said, "with something to eat in it. And you girls had better put on sensible things and cut out the high heels and fancy clothes. If you are going in a street car you'd better be inconspicuous."

That was the way we arranged it finally—the men to take one car and the girls another and meet opposite the island on the river bank. We should have to row across and Ferd was to arrange about boats. We set Thursday as the day.

Some sort of premonition made me nervous— and I was sorry about Day too; for though the picnic was only a lark and no harm at all, of course he would have been furious had he known. And he was very nice to me all the week. He sent flowers home twice and on Wednesday he said I might have a new runabout. That made it rather difficult to quarrel with him Thursday, as I had arranged.

I lay awake half the night trying to think of something to quarrel about. I could not find anything that really answered until nearly dawn, when I decided to give him some bills I had been holding

back. I fell asleep like a child then and did not
waken until eleven o'clock. There was a box of
roses by the bed and a note in Day's writing.

"Honey lamb!" he wrote: "Inclosed is a telegram
from Waite calling me to Newburyport to the tournament. I'll hardly get back before to-morrow
night. I came to tell you, but you looked so beautiful and so sound asleep I did not have the heart
to waken you. Be a good girl! DAY."

Somehow the note startled me. Could he have
had any suspicion? I felt queer and uneasy all the
time I was dressing; but after I had had a cup of
tea I felt better. There is nothing underhanded
about Day. He has no reserves. And if he had
learned about the picnic he would have been bleating
all over the place.

The weather was splendid—a late summer day,
not too warm, with a September haze over everything. We met at the hairdresser's and Jane Henderson was frightfully nervous.

"Of course I'm game," she said, while the man
pinned on her net; "but my hands are like ice."

Catherine, however, was fairly radiant.

"There's a sort of thrill about doing something
clandestine," she observed, "that isn't like anything

else in the world. I feel like eloping with Mr. Lee.
You'll all be mad about him. He's the nicest
thing!"

Mr. Lee was the Moores' guest.

I had got into the spirit of the thing by that time
and I drew a long breath. Day was safely out of
the way, the weather was fine, and I had my hair
over my ears the way Ferd liked it.

II

Everything went wonderfully—up to a certain
point. Have you ever known it to fail? Everything swims along and all is lovely—and the thing,
whatever it may be, is being so successful that it
is almost a culmination; and then suddenly, out
of a clear sky, there is a slip-up somewhere and you
want to crawl off into a corner and die.

Ferd had got there early and had a boat ready,
all scrubbed out and lined with old carpets. He was
just as excited as any of us.

"The trouble with us," he said, as we rowed over
to the island, "is that we are all in a rut. We do
the same things over and over, at the same places,
with the same people. The *hoi polloi* never make
that mistake and they get a lot more out of life.
Every now and then the puddlers from the mill
come over here and have a great time."

There were two islands, one just above the other, with about a hundred feet of water between them. The upper island was much the nicer and it was there that Ferd had planned the party.

He does things awfully well, really. He had had a decorator out there early in the day and the pavilion was fixed up with plants and vines which looked as if they grew on it. He had the table fixed too, with a mound of roses and the most interesting place cards. Mine had a little jewelled dagger thrust through it, and the card said:

That's as much as to say, they are fools that marry.

He said the quotation was from Shakespeare and the dagger was for Day.

Annette's card said:

She was married, charming, chaste, and twenty-three,

which delighted Annette, she being more than twenty-three.

Ferd's own card said:

Another woman now and then
Is relished by the best of men.

I have forgotten the others. The dagger was a pin, and each card had something pretty fastened to it.

We sat and gossiped while we waited for the others and then we wandered round. The island was not very pretty—flat and weedy mostly, with a good many cans the campers had left, and a muddy shore where a broken dock, consisting of two planks on poles, was the boat landing. But it was only later that I hated it, really. That afternoon we said it was idyllic, and the very place for a picnic.

The other men arrived soon after, and it was really barrels of fun. We made a rule first. No one was to mention an absent husband or wife; and the person who did had to tell a story or sing a song as a forfeit. I was more than proud of Ferd. He had even had a phonograph sent up, with a lot of new music. We danced the rest of the afternoon and the Lee man danced like an angel. I never had a better time. Jane voiced my feelings perfectly.

"It's not that I'm tired of Bill," she said. "I dote on him, of course; but it is a relief, once in a while, not to have a husband in the offing, isn't it? And the most carping critic could not object to anything we are doing. That's the best of all."

The dinner was really wonderful—trust Ferd for that too. We were almost hilarious. Between courses we got up and changed our own plates, and we danced to the side table and back again. Once we had an alarm, however. An excursion boat came up the river and swung in close to the pavilion. We had not noticed it until it was quite near and there was no time to run; so we all sat down on the floor inside the railing, which was covered with canvas, and had our salad there.

By the time dinner was over it was almost dark; and we took a bottle of champagne down to the dock and drank it there, sitting on the boards, with our feet hanging. Ferd had been growing sentimental for the last hour or two and I had had to keep him down. He sat beside me on the boards and kept talking about how he envied Day, and that Ida was a good wife and better than he deserved; but no one had ever got into him the way I had.

"I'm not trying to flatter you, Fanny," he said. "I've always been honest with you. But there's a woman for every man, and you're my woman."

He had come rather close and, anyhow, he was getting on my nerves; so I gave him just the least little bit of a push and he fell right back into the water. I was never so astonished in my life.

The way Jane Henderson told it later was criminally false. I did not push him with all my strength and he had not tried to kiss me. Nobody had had too much to drink. It was a perfectly proper party, and my own mother could not have found a single thing to criticise.

Well, Ferd was wet through and not very agreeable. He said, however, that he had merely overbalanced, and that he would dry out somehow. The only thing was that he had to get back home and he felt he was not looking his best.

The moon came up and was perfectly lovely; but about the time we had settled down to singing soft little songs and the Lee man was saying what a good lot of sports we were, and that he was going to take the idea back home, a lot of puddlers and their wives rowed out from the shore and started toward our island. Ferd was awfully annoyed. He stood up and shouted at them.

"You can't come here!" he called. "This place is taken. Go to the other island."

"Go to the devil!" one of the puddlers bellowed from the boat; nevertheless they turned the boat's nose round and went to the other island. We could hear them yelling and laughing there, and singing in the commonest fashion. It ruined the moonlight for us. From that time the bloom was off, as one may say, and things went from bad to worse.

The last car went at ten o'clock, and at half-past nine we commenced to pack up. Annette insisted on taking the roses; and there was the phonograph and the club's silver and dishes, and almost a boatload of stuff. We could not all get in, of course, so Ferd and Emerson Riley agreed to wait; but just as I got into the boat I dropped my gold bag overboard.

I would not go without the bag. It was set with diamonds and I did not know when I should get another. I just got out of the boat and refused to stir until it had been fished out.

There was a great deal of excitement. The last car had come and was waiting on the bank for its return trip, and every one was anxious to get off. Ferd, who was wet anyway, waded in, but he could not locate it immediately, and Jane grew hysterical.

"Come on and leave it, Fan!" she begged. "What's a bag compared with one's reputation? That car's moving now!"

"Go on!" I said coldly. "I shall stay here until Ferd finds it. Go on, all of you! You can send a man back with the boat, I dare say."

They did it! I never was more astounded in my life; but they all piled in except Ferd and me, and made for the shore as fast as they could. They said it was all well enough for me, with Day out of town; but the rest of them never had any luck and they had to get that car.

"They're terribly nervous, all at once!" I said. "If that car goes without me, Ferd, I shall jump into the river!"

It was moonlight, but not very bright. I sat on the dock and Ferd fished for the gold bag. He brought up an empty bottle, two tin cans and an old shoe.

"Look here, Fan," he said finally, "I'll buy you a new bag. I'll do anything—only let's get out of this."

"Try once more."

"I'll get neuralgia," he said. "I have to be awfully careful, Fanny. Ida·has to watch me like a hawk."

"I should imagine so," I replied coldly.

"I mean about the neuralgia."

"Humph! Day never has anything the matter with him—that's one thing. Try again, Ferd."

He stooped again, and this time he got it. He straightened up with it in his hand. The car was still on the bank and a boat was putting out from the shore. All seemed to be well.

"They'll bribe the motorman to wait," said Ferd. "I told Riley to. So you see, little girl, everything's all right. Here's the bag and there's the boat. Do you like me a little bit again?"

I felt rather queer, alone there on the island with him; and the only thing that occurred to me was to keep him down.

"I'll like you well enough when we get back to civilization," I said shortly.

"You're not like yourself, Fanny. You aren't a bit kind to me."

"Being nice to you with everybody round is one thing. This is another. I'm scared, Ferd."

"Not of me!" he said, getting hold of one of my hands. He looked horrid in the moonlight, with his collar in a crease and his coat stuck to him. He looked awfully thin, too, and his hair was in straggles over his face. "Fan, the boat's coming and I never see you alone. Do say you care a little bit!"

Well, I had to play the game. I am not a quitter. I had let him get up the party and spend a lot of money, and I had pretended for months to be interested in him. What was I to do? You. may say what you like—a lot of married women get into things they never meant to simply because they are kind-hearted and hate to be called quitters.

"I've always cared a little," I said, trying not to look at him. "Ferd, you're dripping! Don't touch me!"

"Lady-love!" cried Ferd, very close to my ear; and then: "Good gracious, Fan! Where's the boat?"

It had absolutely disappeared! Ferd stood up on the shaky dock and peered over the water.

"He's gone to the other island," he said after a moment. "They'll tell him he's wrong, but—time's passing!"

He did not start the lady-love business again, and we sat side by side on the dock, with the river, damp and smelly, underfoot. It was very silent, save for the far-away yells of the puddlers on the next island and the drip-drip from Ferd's trouser-ends to the water below.

Somehow the snap was gone out of the whole thing. I hated it, being alone with him there, and his looking so mussy, and my vanity case soaking from the river. I hated the puddlers' picnic; there was nothing I didn't hate. And the boatman did not come. Even Ferd began to get anxious.

"The infernal fool!" he said. "He's probably joined the picnic, and—— Hello, there!" he called, with his hands to his mouth.

I think they heard us on the bank, for we could hear the trolley bell very faintly. And, immediately after, the car moved off! I had the most awful feeling. We sat on the boards watching it getting smaller and smaller down the river, and neither of us said anything. It had been our one tie, as you may say, to respectability and home—and it had deserted us. After a minute Ferd got up on his feet.

"It's the puddlers, after all!" he said. "We'll have to hail them and get them to send that ass of a boatman. Wouldn't you think that Emerson Riley would have had sense enough to wait and see that we got over safely?"

I fairly clutched at his arm.

"You'll do nothing of the sort," I said. "They'll know you if they're from your mill, and they'll know I am not Ida! It will be in the papers!"

Ferd looked sulky.

"What am I to do, then?" he demanded. "Swim to the bank?"

"Couldn't you swim to the other island and steal one of their boats?"

He did not want to. I could see that; but what else was there to do?

"It's a good way off," he said. "It won't help things any for me to be drowned, you know."

"It would be better than a scandal, wouldn't it?"

He threw up his hands.

"Oh, if that's the way you feel——"

"That isn't half the way I feel!"

He went off at that in a fury, leaving me alone on the little dock in a state of frenzy. I kept thinking of Day's getting home sooner than he expected and finding me gone, and calling up the police; and my wandering in about daylight with my slippers worn through. I made up a story—if the worst happened—about having had an attack of loss of memory, coming to myself seven miles from town and walking in.

There was no sign of Ferd. The puddlers' picnic

was noisier than ever; they had brought a phonograph, too, and were dancing.

When I had waited for what seemed half the night I got frightened about Ferd. He had said it was a good way to go; and if he was drowned—and Ida really fond of him, and welcome to him so far as I was concerned—it was all up with me. Day would loathe the very sight of me. I knew that.

The grass looked snaky in the moonlight and I felt I was taking my life in my hands; but, somehow or other, with my hair pulled down by branches, and ankle-deep in mud every now and then, I got to the place where the two islands faced each other, end to end. There was not a sign of Ferd.

I just sank down on the ground and hoped for death. There was no way out. Jane and the others would think we had the boat and could hire a machine or something to get to the city, and they would not give us another thought. Even if I hailed the puddlers and told them, they would never believe my story. And, of course, there was poor Ferd in the river mud—sure to float in and spoil any story I could make up about loss of memory.

It was when I had reached that point that pandemonium broke loose on the other island. I could hear shouting—men and women together—and, in a pause, the frantic splashing of oars. The next moment a boat appeared round the corner of the island, with Ferd rowing like mad, and a perfect pandemonium from the shore. He had stolen their boat and they had found it out. I was almost crazy. I waded out to my knees and called to him; and he saw me. There was no other boat after him yet, but some one was yelling to follow him.

Ferd was rather steadied by the excitement, I think. He reached over and dragged me in without a word, and the next instant we were pulling for the shore in the moonlight, with the entire puddlers' picnic on their bank, calling awful things to us.

That was not all, though. One of the men had got into their other boat and was coming after us. He could row, too. I implored Ferd to hurry—hurry. And I kept turning round to see whether he was gaining. That was how I discovered why they were so wrought up. There were two dozen quart bottles of champagne in the stern of that boat! We were carrying off the picnic! I told Ferd. "Throw it overboard!" he said. "It'll lighten the boat."

So I did, basket after basket; and, whether it lightened the boat or not, we drew ahead. Ferd rowed like a demon. In the moonlight his face was white and set, with the queerest expression.

We struck the shore with a bump that sent me on

my knees, but Ferd grabbed my hand and jerked me out.

"Now run—if you ever ran in your life!" he said. "Make for that grove over there, and bend over. The bushes will hide us."

"I can't," I panted after a minute. "And why should I, Ferd? He's got his old boat by this time——"

"Run!" gasped Ferd. And I ran.

We crouched down in the grove. My teeth were chattering, but I was nothing to Ferd. He was pallid. The puddler landed just then. We heard him throw his oars into the boat and drag it up on the beach, and I knew he was examining the other boat and finding that the wine was gone. We could hear him breathing hard, and he even made a start toward us, beating the bushes with an oar. He was in a red fury, muttering to himself in the most horrible manner. I had been in Ferd's mill once or twice, and I remembered the enormous shoulders the men had, and how they simply toyed with steel rails; and I was paralysed. A puddler turned Berserk!

He gave it up just in time, however, and started back for the boat. I could see him moving about— a huge creature in white flannels. And he seemed to have cut himself on a branch or something, for he was tying a handkerchief round his forehead.

We did not dare to move until he had started back and was safely out from shore. Ferd's voice had lost its strained quality and he looked a little less like death. We could hear the picnic party calling to the man in the boat about the wine, and his calling back that we had got away with it, but for some of them to come over and they could beat the bushes. They couldn't come, of course, until he took the boat back.

"We've got to get out of here, Fan," Ferd said. "In ten minutes the whole shooting match will be here. Can you run any more?"

"Not a foot—I'm all in. And I lost a shoe in the water at the island."

Ferd groaned.

"They'll have us up for stealing their champagne," he said. "I suppose you can walk."

"I can limp along, I dare say." I was wet and cold, and horribly miserable. "Don't let me detain you. They can't arrest me for stealing their wine. You did that."

He turned to me suddenly.

"Fan," he said solemnly, "don't ask me why, but we must get out of here quick. Must! If you can't walk, roll. Now come on!"

There were no houses in sight. The trolley line ends there, and I think it is a picnic grove. He took my hand and dragged me along. I lost my other slipper, but he paid no attention when I told him of it; and just when I was about to sink down and die we reached a road.

"Now," said Ferd, "they came in something—machines probably—for they'll have to get back, and there are no more cars. Ah, there they are!"

There were two machines. I gripped Ferd's arm and held him back desperately.

"The chauffeurs?" I gasped.

"We'll kill 'em, if necessary," he said between clenched teeth.

We were loping down the road toward the machines—Ferd sloshing, rather, with each step; and we could hear loud calling from the islands and the banging of oars in oarlocks.

"F-Ferd," I managed to say, "c-can—you—drive—a—car?"

"Why, you can, can't you?"

"I—can—d-drive—my—own car. I d-don't—know about—any other."

"They're all alike. The principle's the same."

"I don't know anything about the principles," I said despairingly. "And I won't touch a strange machine."

"Oh, very well!" said Ferd sulkily. "We'll make a deuce of a stir—arrested here for stealing a case of champagne; but never mind. It'll blow over."

"We can tell the whole story."

"We cannot!" he said gloomily. "We can't tell on Jane and Annette and Catherine. We'll have to take our medicine, that's all. We needn't give our own names. That's one thing."

I was perfectly crazed with fright and exhaustion. I leaned up against a fence, and I remembered the time Lily Slater asked Ollie Haynes to see her off to Chicago, her husband being out of town; and how Ollie was carried two hundred miles before the train would stop to let him off; and how Harry never believed the story and was off shooting big game at that very minute; and Lily getting gray over her ears as a result, and not even going out to lunch with anybody for fear there were detectives watching her.

And, compared with Day, Harry Slater was an angel of mildness.

The boat was almost across by that time and Ferd was wringing the ends of his trousers. A sort of frenzy seized me. It seemed to me it would be better to be found crushed under a strange car than to be arrested for stealing champagne. I started on, rather tottery.

"I'll try it, Ferd," I said. "I think we'll be killed; but come on!"

For once luck was with us. It was a car exactly like my own! I almost cried for joy. I leaped in and pressed the starter, and the purr of the engine was joyous, absolutely. I let in the clutch and the darling slid along without a jerk. We were saved! I could drive that car. I snapped the gear lever forward into high and the six cylinders leaped to our salvation. We were off, with the white road ahead; and the puddlers were only beaching their boat. Ferd sat half turned and watched for pursuit.

"They'll search the bushes first," he said. "They'll not think of the machines for a few minutes. We can hit it up along the highway for four or five miles; then we'd better turn into a side road and put out the lights and take off the license plates. They'll telephone ahead possibly and give the license number."

We were going pretty fast by that time and just at that moment I saw a buggy ahead in the road. Ferd called to me; but it was too late—I had pressed the siren and the very hills echoed.

"Good heavens, Fan!" he said. "You've done it now!"

We topped a rise just then and Ferd looked back. The puddlers were running along the road toward the place where they had left their cars. It was a race for life after that. Ferd bent over and pressed the button that put out the tail light, and I threw on all the gas I could.

"It's getting pretty serious," Ferd said. "We'll go

up for a year or two for this, probably. Stealing a machine is no joke."

"If it comes to that I'll steer the thing over a bank and die with it!" I said, with my jaw set. "Ferd, there's something wrong somewhere! Listen to that knocking!"

The engine was not behaving well. It was not hitting right and it was telling on our speed. As we topped a long rise Ferd saw the lights of another car appear over the crest of the last hill. Down in the valley ahead lay a village, sound asleep. We raced through it like mad. A man in his shirt-sleeves rushed out of a house and yelled something to us about stopping, that we were under arrest. We almost went over him.

The race would be over soon, that was clear. The car was making time, but not better time than the other machine. I do not know how I got the idea, but we went limping and banging along until we had reached the edge of the town, and just beyond, beside the road, was a barn, with the doors open. I turned the car in there, shut off the engine and put out the lamps. Ferd caught the idea at once and leaped out and closed the doors.

"Good girl!" he said. "Unless the farmer heard us and comes out to investigate, this is pretty snug, lady-love. They'll pass us without even hesitating."

They did not, though. It gives me gooseflesh

merely to remember the next half-hour. We waited
inside the door for the car to pass. We could hear
it coming. But just at the barn it stopped and we
could hear them arguing. It seems the road forked
there and they were not certain which way we had
gone. My knees were shaking with terror and Ferd
was breathing hard.

When I look back I think I should have noticed
how queer Ferd was during the whole thing; and,
when you think of it, why did he steal the boat at
the beginning and not just borrow it? But I was
absolutely unsuspicious; and as for noticing, there
was no time.

I lost my courage, I'll admit, when they stopped;
and I ran to the back of the barn. There was a horse
there and I squeezed in beside the thing; it was company anyhow and not running about the country trying to arrest people who were merely attempting to
get home. It seemed uneasy and I tried to pat its
head to soothe it—and it had horns! I almost
fainted. Somehow or other I climbed out, and Ferd
was coming toward me.

"Sh!" he whispered. "They've roused the farmer,
and—holy smoke!—they're coming in!"

Somebody had opened one of the doors about six
inches. That made a path of moonlight across the
board floor.

"I dunno why they closed the barn doors to-night," said the farmer from the opening—"mostly we leave 'em open. Now, gentlemen, if you want water for your automobile there's a pail inside the door here, and the pump's round the corner in the pig yard."

Fred clutched my arm. The moonlight path was slowly widening as the door swung open. "Quick!" he said; and the next minute I was climbing a ladder to the haymow, with Ferd at my heels.

One thing saved us and one only: the farmer did not come inside to see the car; and whoever did come clearly thought it belonged to the place and never even glanced at it. As for us we lay face down in that awful haymow with openings in the hay big enough to fall through, and watched and listened. I shall never be the same person again after that experience.

Whenever I get cocky, as Day would say, and reflect on my own virtues, and how few things I do that any one could find fault with, not playing bridge for more than two and a half cents a point, and stopping a flirtation before it reaches any sort of gossipy stage, I think of Ferd and myself in that awful haymow, with a man below searching round that miserable machine for a pail, and Ferd oozing a slow drip-drip on the floor below that was enough to give us away—like the blood dropping from the ceiling in that play of David Belasco's.

There was one awful moment before it was all over, when the farmer had gone back to bed and the man returned the pail. The others were all in their machine, yelling to be off.

"They've had time to be gone twenty miles," one of them snarled. "The next time we see them, shoot at their tires. It's the only way."

The man with the pail stood in the doorway and glanced in.

"Pipe the car!" he said. "The farmers are the only folks with real money these days."

He came in with the pail and one of the drops from Ferd's clothes hit him directly on top of the head! I heard it spat! He stopped as if he had been shot and looked up. I closed my eyes and waited for the end; but—nothing happened. He put away the pail and hurried out, and the machine went on.

It was Ferd who spoke first. He raised himself on an elbow and listened. Then he drew a long breath, as if he had not breathed for an hour.

"Well," he said, "I may not be a thief and a robber, as well as an abductor of young married women, but I feel like one." He looked about the haymow, and at me, crumpled in my corner. "Really, you know," he said, "this sort of thing isn't done, Fanny."

"If it only doesn't get into the papers!" I wailed.

"And if only Day doesn't hear of it! Ferd, I must look a mess."

He glanced at me. The moonlight was coming through a window.

"You do look rather frowzy," he said.

I think, if there is a psychological moment for such things, that was the moment. My affair, mild as it was, was dead from that instant. Day would never have said such a thing. Day never takes his irritation out on me; the worse I look the more certain Day is to reassure me. For instance, Day never says that—to him—I am as pretty as the day he first met me. He says that I am prettier than I ever was, and that every one thinks so. Day has a positive talent for being married.

Well, we sat in the haymow and quarrelled. We thought it best to let them go on, give up the search and go back to the island for their women companions, before venturing out. So we sat and fought.

"It was stupid," I said, "to have stolen the boat and not borrowed it."

"I'd have had to explain you," said Ferd.

"You need not have mentioned me. What is a lie for, if not for such an emergency? Couldn't you have found that boatman? That would have explained everything."

"I couldn't find the boatman."

"Did you try?"

He turned sulky.

"I did my best," he said. "I risked my life. I'll probably have a sick spell as it is. I've got a chill. How did I know the infernal boat had champagne in it?"

I sat and thought. A lot of things came to me that I had not thought of before, such as Ferd having got up the party and put me in my present position, and having been a stupid in more ways than one. And what if Day had got home unexpectedly? I said this to Ferd.

"Why didn't you think of that sooner?" he demanded brutally.

"What time is it?" I asked, as sweetly as I could.

He held his watch up in the moonlight, but of course it was full of water and not running. His matches and cigarettes were wet, too, and he grew more beastly every minute.

"Ferd," I said finally, "I'm afraid lately you've been thinking that I—that I cared for you. It was my fault. I let you think so. I don't, really. I only care for one man and I think you ought to know it. I've been a shameless flirt. That's all."

Instead of being downcast, he rather brightened up at that remark.

"You'll break my heart if you say that," he said, trying not to be too cheerful.

"There's only one man for me!" I said firmly.

"It's not fashionable, but it's very comforting. It's Day."

"I'll never be the same man again, Fanny," he replied. "Am I not to call you up, or send you flowers, or look forward to seeing you at the Country Club on Sunday afternoons? Is life to lose all its joy?"

"Oh, we'll have to meet, of course," I said largely; "but—the other is off for good, Ferd! I find I can't stand too much of you. You're too heady."

Well, he was almost blithe over it, and sat talking about Ida, and what a trump she was about the time he lost so much on copper, and the way she came home from Nice when he had typhoid. It was stupid; but if you can understand me it seemed to put a cachet of respectability on our position. The more we talked about Day and Ida, the more we felt that the tongue of scandal could never touch us. We made a pact of platonic friendship, too, and shook hands on it; and it shows how dead the old affair was when Ferd never even kissed my hand.

About an hour afterward the other car went back toward the island and we got up stiffly and crawled down the ladder. Ferd had had a nap, and he slept with his mouth open!

We slipped out of the barn in the moonlight and reconnoitered. There was no one in sight and the house across the road was dark. Ferd took off the license plates and put them under one of the seat cushions and I looked for the short circuit. I found it at last, and Ferd fixed it with his pen-knife. Then he threw the doors open and we backed into the road. The last thing I remember is that as we started off a window was raised in the farmhouse and somebody yelled after us to stop.

"Damnation!" said Ferd between his teeth. "He'll telephone ahead and they'll cut us off!"

"We needn't stick to the main road. We can go back through the country."

We found a lane leading off half a mile farther along and I turned into it. It was rough, but its very condition argued for safety. As Ferd said, no one in his sane mind would choose such a road. The secret of the lane came out a mile or so farther on, however, when it came to an end in a barnyard. It was a blow, really. We did not dare to go back and we could not possibly go ahead.

"I can go up to the house and ask about the road," Ferd said. "The old stage road ought to be round here somewhere. If we can't find it there's nothing to do but to walk, Fan."

"I can't walk," I said, "and I won't walk. I'm in my stocking feet. I'm through. Let's just go back and get arrested and have it over. I can't stand much more."

"It's only twelve miles or so to town."

"I couldn't walk twelve miles to escape hanging!"

Ferd crawled out of the car and through a pig yard. I heard the pigs squealing. And then for five awful minutes I heard nothing except his distant knock and muffled voices. Then there was a silence, and out of it came Ferd headlong. He fell over the fence and landed in the mud beside the car.

"Quick!" he panted. "Turn round and get back to the main road. They've got him on the telephone, and in another minute———"

Did you ever try to turn an automobile in a panic and a small barnyard, with broken mowing machines and old wagons everywhere? I just could not do it. I got part way round, with Ferd begging me for Heaven's sake to get some speed on, when we heard people coming from the house on a run, and a woman yelling from a window that she could see us and to shoot quick.

There was a field next the barnyard—a pasture, I suppose—and the bars were down that led into it. I just headed the car for it and shut my eyes. Then we were shooting forward in a series of awful bumps, with Ferd holding on with both hands, and the noise behind was dying away.

I do not recall the details of that part of the trip. Ferd says we went through two creeks and a small woods, and entirely through and over a barbed-wire fence, which was probably where we got our punctures. However that may be, in five minutes or so we drew up just inside a fence on the other side of which was a road. And we had two flat tires.

Ferd tried to take the fence down, but he could not; so I did the only thing I could think of, and butted it down with the car. The glass in the lamps was smashed, but we were too far gone by that time to care. I had just one thought; if the gas only held out!

Ferd was quite sure he knew the way to town, but it turned out he did not. For hours and hours we bumped along on two tires and two rims, until my shoulders felt torn from their sockets. The worst of it was the noise we made. Every now and then we passed a farmhouse where the lights were going and everybody had been roused for the automobile thieves; and, instead of slipping past, we bumped by like a circus parade with a calliope.

The moon was gone by that time; and, our lamps being broken, more than once we left the road entirely and rolled merrily along in a field until we brought up against something. And, of course, we met a car. We heard it coming, but there was nothing to do but bump along. It was a limousine, and it hailed us and drew up so we could not pass.

"In trouble?" a man called.

"Nothing serious," Ferd said peevishly.

"Glad to give you a hand. You're cutting your tires to bits."

"No; thanks."

"I can take you back to town if you like."

It was Bill Henderson, Jane's husband, on his way from the club to his mother's in the country! I could not even breathe. Ferd knew it too, that minute.

"We are getting along all right," he snapped, trying to disguise his voice. "If you'll get your car out of the way——"

"Oh, all right, Ferd, old chap!" said Bill, and signalled his man to go on.

We sat as if petrified. Bill was Ida's cousin! The way of the transgressor is hard; though why one should have to lose a reputation built up by years of careful living just for one silly indiscretion is what gets me. I put a hand on Ferd's arm.

"I'm gone!" I wailed. "It will be all over town to-morrow. Bill's the worst old gossip. Oh, Ferd!"

"He didn't see you," Ferd snapped. "For goodness' sake, Fan, shut up! This is my mess. There isn't any limit to the things he can say about me."

We bumped on a little farther. I was crying, I'll admit; my head ached and my spine was jarred numb.

"You'll have to do one thing," he said at last.

"You'll have to tell Ida it was you. Heaven knows what she'll think."

"I'll die first!" I snapped.

Well, we got into town finally and it was three-thirty by the first clock we saw. Ferd got out and looked at the car, and then climbed in again.

"Better get along a few blocks and then leave it," he said. "It looks something fierce, and so do we."

And at that instant, before I could even start the engine, we were arrested for stealing the miserable thing!

"There is some mistake," Ferd said loftily, but looking green in the electric light. "This is Mrs. Day Illington and this is her own machine."

"Are you Mr. Illington?"

"Yes!" said Ferd.

The man looked very strange, as well he might, considering—well, considering the facts that came out later.

"I'll have to trouble you to come with me," he said, politely enough. "It will be only a short delay and we'll get this straightened out. But a car answering this description was stolen out the road a few miles and headed toward town, and there's a reward offered."

He stood on the step and I drove to the station house. I had it fixed in my own mind to go home and write a letter to Day confessing all, and then pack a few things and hide my wretched self for the rest of my life. I even planned what to take; my jewelry and my checkbook, and only a dinner dress or two; and I wrote the letter to Day—in my mind—and one to Ida, telling her it was only a lark, but it had gone wrong without any fault of mine. Then we drew up at the station.

Ferd got out and went in, and the officer turned on the pavement to help me out. But it was my chance and I took it; I just threw on the gas full and shot ahead down the street. He yelled after me and then began shooting. One bullet must have struck the good rear tire, for it collapsed and almost turned the car round. But I was desperate. I never looked back. I just drove for all I was worth down the street to its end, and after that down other streets, and still others. All the time I was saying I would rather die, and going round corners on two wheels, or one wheel and a rim.

Finally I got into a part of town I knew and pulled up half a block from my own house. I recall that and leaving the engine still going, and that hideous nightmare of a machine standing by the curb, with its tires lying out on the road in ribbons and its lamps smashed; and I remember going up the steps and finding the hall door unlocked. Then I recall nothing more for a while. I fainted.

It was Martha, one of the housemaids, who found

me, I believe, as she was going out to early mass. They got me upstairs to bed and there was no use trying to run away that night; I could hardly stand. They got me some hot tea and a doctor and a trained nurse, and in the morning before breakfast Day came back. He tiptoed into my room and tried to kiss me, looking awfully frightened; but I would not let him.

"Send the nurse out!" I whispered. So he did; and still I would not let him kiss me. "Not until I've told you something," I said feebly. "You may not care to when you've heard it all."

He looked so big and so dependable and so worried that I could have screamed; but I had to tell him. Bill Henderson might have recognised me; and Ferd, as like as not, would be goose enough to tell Ida the whole story. And, anyhow, there's nothing like perfect honesty between husband and wife.

"Day," I said tremulously, "I'm a felon—a thief! I—I stole a lot of champagne last night and an automobile, and broke down fences, and almost ran over a policeman, and was arrested—or Ferd was—Day, don't look like that!" For his face was terrible. He had gone quite white.

"You!" he said.

"Get up and stand by the window, looking out," I implored him. "I can tell you better if I can't see your eyes."

So he did and I told him the whole thing. He never moved, and I kept getting more and more frightened. It sounded worse, somehow, when I told it. When I had finished he did not come to me as I had hoped. He said:

"I'd like a few minutes to get used to it, Fan. I'll go out and walk about a bit. It's—it's just a little hard to grasp, all at once."

So he went out, and I lay and cried into my pillow; but when the nurse had brought me some tea and raised the shades, and the sun came in, I felt a little better. He had not been noisy, anyhow; and in time perhaps he would forgive me, though probably he would never really trust me again. I got up in a chair and had my hair tied with a ribbon and my nails done, and put on my new negligee with lace sleeves; and I felt pretty well, considering.

At nine o'clock the policeman on the beat asked to see me. I sent down word that I was indisposed; but he said it was urgent and would only take a moment. The nurse put a blanket over my knees and a pillow behind me, and the officer came in. I was frightened; but after all my only real fear had been Day, and now that he knew, Fate could hardly have a fresh blow. But it had, all right.

"Sorry to disturb you, ma'am," said the officer, "but it's about your car."

"Yes?" My lips were trembling.

"It's been found; I found it—and only a block or so away, ma'am; but it's in bad shape—lamps smashed and tires chewed to ribbons. It's a sight, for sure!"

"But that's not my car!" I exclaimed, forgetting caution.

"I guess there's no mistake about it, ma'am. Those fellows that stole it, up the river, must have climbed fences with it."

"How do you know it is my car?" I was absolutely bewildered.

"These are your license plates, aren't they? I found them under the seat."

They were my license plates!

Day came in shortly after and tiptoed into the room. The nurse was out. He came over to me and stooped down.

"It took me a little by surprise, honey," he said; "but that's over now. You've been foolish, but you've had your lesson. Let's kiss and be friends again."

"Just a moment, Day," I said calmly. "Have you had your lesson?"

"Just what do you mean?"

He followed my eyes to the table and the license plates were there. He actually paled.

"Where did you get them?"

"Under the seat of the car Ferd and I stole last night at Devil's Island—my car, which you said was being overhauled!"

He drew a long breath. Then he got down on his knees and put his head in my lap.

"I've had my lesson—honest, honey!" he said. "Some darned fool suggested a picnic on one of those islands—mixed couples—and I was ass enough to agree. I took Ida Jackson. We didn't have any picnic—the champagne was stolen——"

"Ferd and I——" I put in.

"And then my car went——"

"My car—and I took it."

"And we spent all the evening and part of the night chasing the thing for fear you'd hear of it!" He looked up at me and there were dark circles round his eyes. "I haven't been to bed at all, honey," he said humbly. "It's been a rotten night! I've had enough affinity for the rest of my life. There's nobody like you!"

I would not kiss him just then, but I let him lie down on my couch and hold my hand until he dropped asleep. Somehow the words of Ferd's silly card kept running through my head:

> *Another woman now and then*
> *Is relished by the best of men.*

My little affair with Ferd had seemed harmless enough and the picnic had been a lark; but Day and Ida had had a picnic and it had been a lark—only the shoe was on the other foot, and it hurt!

And somehow, as I sat there, it seemed to me that the affinity business was only fun because it was dangerous. We were all children, and life was a Fourth of July, enchanting because it was risky.

Day was sleeping, with his mouth shut! I leaned over and kissed him as he dozed.

Sitting there, with Day asleep, I went over the events of the night, and I knew that Ferd had had his lesson, too, and that, having been burnt, he would not play with fire again—at least not until the blister had healed; for Ferd had seen the island picnickers and had learned that they were not puddlers. He had seen Ida and Day and, worst of all, he had known that it was Day who was pursuing us.

I thought of that hour in the haymow, with Day and the others below, and Ferd dripping; and very quietly, so as not to waken my husband, I went into a paroxysm of mirth.

THE FAMILY FRIEND

THE FAMILY FRIEND

I

I'VE thought the thing over and over, and honestly I don't know where it went wrong. It began so well. I planned it out, and it went exactly as I'd expected up to a certain point. Then it blew up.

There's no argument about it, a girl has to look out for herself. The minute the family begin mixing in there's trouble.

The day after I came out mother and I had a real heart-to-heart talk. I'd been away for years at school, and in the summers we hadn't seen much of each other. She played golf all day and I had my tennis and my horse. And in the evenings there were always kid dances. So we really got acquainted that day.

She rustled into my room and gazed at what was left of my ball gown, spread out on the bed.

"It really went rather well last night," she said.

"Yes, mother," I replied.

"I've sent the best of the flowers to the hospital."

"Yes, mother."

"You had more flowers than Bessie Willing."

I shrugged my shoulders, and for some reason or other that irritated her.

"For heaven's sake, Kit," she said sharply, "I wish you'd show a little appreciation. Your father has spent a fortune on you, one way and another. The supper alone last night—— But that's not what I came to talk about."

"No, mother?"

"No. Are you going to continue to waste your time on Henry Baring?"

"I rather enjoy playing round with him. That's all it amounts to."

"Not at all," said mother in her best manner. "It keeps the others away."

"As, for instance?" I asked politely.

She was getting on my nerves. I didn't mean to marry Henry, but I did mean to carry on my own campaign.

"You know very well that there are only three marriageable men in town. There are eleven débutantes. And—I don't care to be unkind, but at least four of them are—are——"

"I know," I said wearily—"better looking than I am. Go ahead."

"You're not at all ugly," mother put in hastily. "A great many people said nice things about you last night. The only thing I want to impress on you is that Madge will have to come out next year, and that you've been reared with expensive tastes."

"I've got brains. Most of the other eleven haven't."

"Brains are a liability, not an asset."

"That's an exploded idea, mother. The only times they are a liability is when they are ruined by too much family interest."

"That sounds impertinent," she said coldly.

"Not at all; it's good business. If I'm to put over anything worth while, I shall have to work along my own lines. I can't afford to have my style cramped."

She raised her eyebrows at that, for she hates slang. But she looked relieved too. When I think of how sure of myself I was that day I could rave!

"Then you're not going to waste any more time on Henry?"

"I think," I said reflectively, "that I'm going to use Henry quite a lot. But I don't intend to marry him."

Yes, that's what I said. I remember it perfectly well. I was putting a dab of scent behind my ears at the time. I feel that I shall never use the stuff again.

Well, mother went out quite cheered. It was the first real mother-and-daughter talk we'd had for a long time. When she had gone I went into my bathroom and locked the door and opened the windows and smoked two cigarettes, thinking things out.

The family is opposed to my smoking, and no one knows except mother's maid, who fixes my hair, and the gardener. When for the third time he had seen smoke coming out of my bathroom window, and had rushed upstairs with a fire grenade and all the servants at his heels, I was compelled to take him into my confidence.

Well, I smoked and thought things out. I am not beautiful, but I'm extremely *chic*, and at night, with a touch of rouge, I do very well. I have always worn sophisticated clothes. I thought they suited my style. But so did all the others. If I was to do anything distinguished it would have to be on new lines.

"Early Victorian?" I said to myself.

But the idea of me Lydia-languishing, prunes-and-prisming round the place was too much.

Athletics? Well, they were not bad. There's a lot of chance in golf, although tennis is blowzy. I look well in sport clothes too. But if a girl is a dub at a game a man is apt to tell her so, and I know my own disposition. If he criticised me, before I knew it I'd be swatting my prey with a mashie or a niblick, and everything over. Three men, mother had said. I knew who they were. They had all sent me flowers and danced with me, without saying a word, and then taken me back to mother and rushed for the particular married woman they were interested in.

Oh, I'm not blind! All the men I knew, old enough to amount to anything, were interested in some married woman. I drive my own car, and I used to meet them on lonely back roads, Lillian Marshall and Tom Connor, Toots Warrington and Russell Hill, and the rest of them.

I ask you, what chance had a débutante among them? There were two things to decide that afternoon, the man and the method. I was out now. The family had agreed to let me alone. I had a year before me, until Madge came out. And I knew I could count on Henry Baring to help me all he could. He was a sort of family friend. When he couldn't get me he would take Madge to kid picnics, and mother used to call on him to make a fourth at bridge or fill in at a dinner. You know the sort.

He worked at something or other, and made enough to keep him and pay his club bills, and to let him send flowers to débutantes, and to set up an occasional little supper to pay his way socially. But nobody ever thought of marrying him. He was tall and red-headed and not very handsome. Have I said that?

So I counted on Henry. It makes me bitter even

to write it. His very looks were solid and dependable, although I underestimated his hair. I've said I had brains. Well, I had too many brains. Mother was right—the world doesn't come to the clever folks, it comes to the stubborn, obstinate, one-idea-at-a-time people.

I'm going to tell this thing, because a lot of people are saying I threw away a good thing, and mother——

I have a certain amount of superstition in me. I remember, when I was about to be confirmed at school, I was told to open the Bible at random and take the first verse my eyes fell on for a sort of motto through life. Mine was to the effect that as a partridge sits on eggs and fails to hatch them, so too the person who gets riches without deserving them. It rather bothered me at the time. Well, it never will again.

So I took three cigarettes and marked each one with the initials of an eligible. Then I shook them up in a box and drew Russell Hill. I knew then that I had my work cut out for me. Even with Henry's help it was going to be a hard pull. Russell Hill was spoiled. Probably out of the other eleven at least nine had Russell in the backs of their heads. And he knew every move of the game. They'd all been tried on him—golf and moonlight and 1830 methods and pro and anti suffrage and amateur theatricals and ingénue technique and the come-hither glance. So far they had all failed.

The girls were coming in for tea and to talk things over, and as I dressed I was thinking hard. Mother had gone out for a golf lesson, so I sent the rest of my cigarettes down to the drawing room and picked up a book. I remember only one line of that book. Believe me, as a matrimonial text it had the partridge one going. The girl in the story had been crazy about a man.

"I always had my hand in his coat pocket!" she said.

Don't misunderstand, she was not robbing him. She slipped her hand into his coat pocket to let him know how fond she was of him. And after a moment, she said, he always put his hand in, too, over hers. And he ended her slave. He was a very sophisticated man, up to every move of the game, and he ended her slave!

But Russell would take tact. A man likes to be adored, but he hates to look foolish. The first thing was, of course, to get his attention. I was only one of a dozen. True, he had sent me flowers, but he probably did what all the others did—had a standing order and a box of his cards at the florist's. I wasn't fooled for a minute. To him I was a flapper, nothing else. Whether flapper is a term of reproach or one of tribute depends on whether the girl is a débutante or in the first line of the chorus of a musical show. Oh, I wasn't very old, but I knew my way about.

Margaret North came first and the rest trailed in soon after. Everybody talked about the ball, and said it had been wonderful, and I sat there and sized them up. I had a fight on my hands, and I knew it.

There was a picture of Madge sitting round, and Margaret North picked it up and took it to the light. Margaret is one of the four mother had so delicately referred to.

"You'll have to hurry, Kit," she said. "Sister's a raving beauty."

"Oh, I don't know," I observed casually. "Beauty's not everything.

The girl in the book had not been a beauty.

"It's all there is," said Margaret. "Figure doesn't count any more. Anybody can have a figure who has a decent dressmaker."

"How about brains?" I asked.

There was a squeal at that.

"Cut 'em out," said Ellie Clavering. "Hide 'em. Disguise 'em. Brains are—are clandestine."

"Anyhow," somebody put in, "Kit isn't worrying; she's got Henry."

That's how they'd fixed me. I knew what it meant. It was a cheap game, but they were playing it. They were going to tie me to Henry. They would ask us together, and put us together at dinners, and talk about us together. In the end everybody would think of us together. I'd seen it done before. It's ruined more débutantes than anything else. They'd put me out of the running before I'd started.

I sat back with my cup of tea and listened, and it made me positively ill. It wasn't that they were clever. They were just instinctive. I could have screamed. And having disposed of me, having handcuffed me to Henry Baring and lost the key, so to speak, they went on to the real subject, which was Russell.

Mother had said there were three eligibles. But to those little idiots round the tea table there was only one. They'd been friendly enough as long as Henry and I were on the rack. But the moment Russell's name was mentioned there was a difference. They didn't talk so much and they eyed each other more. Ella Clavering put both lemon and cream in her tea, and drank it without noticing. Somebody said very impressively that she understood the affair with Toots was off, and that Russell had said, according to report, that he was glad of it. He'd have a little time to himself now.

"That means, I dare say," I said languidly, "that

Russell is ready to bring his warmed-over affections to some of us!"

There was a sort of electric silence for a minute.

"It will take a very sophisticated person to land Russell after Toots," I went on. "He's past the ingénue stage."

"If a girl is pretty she always has a chance with Russell." Margaret, of course. She was standing in front of a mirror and I had my eyes on her. Evidently what I had said made an impression, for she cocked her hat down an inch more over her right eye and watched to see the effect.

"You ought to wear earrings, dear," I said. "You need just that dash of *chic*."

Just for a moment I could see in every eye a sort of vision of Toots Warrington, with the large pearls she always wore in her ears—Toots, who had had Russell tame-catting for her off and on for years!

Oh, they fell for it all right! I poured myself another cup of tea to hide the triumph in my face. Little idiots! If he was sick of Toots he'd hate everything that reminded him of her. I could see the crowd of them swaggering in at the next party, in their best imitation of Toots Warrington, with eyes slightly narrowed, and earrings. And I could see Russell's soul turn over in revolt and go out and take a walk. I knew a lot about men even then, but not enough. I know more now.

II

That night Henry Baring came to call. Being a sort of family friend he had a way of walking in unexpectedly, with a box of candy for whoever saw him first. If mother and I were out, he played chess with father. If there was no one in, he was quite likely to range round the lower floor, and ask the butler about his family, and maybe read for an hour or so in the library. The servants adored him, but he was matrimonially impossible.

That night he came. I was at home alone.

"You will take two full days' rest after your ball," mother had said. "I have seen enough débutantes looking ready for the hospital the first week they came out."

So I was alone that evening, and mother and father had gone to a dinner. I was sulky, I don't mind saying. At six o'clock a box of flowers had come, but they were only from Henry and not exciting. "Thought I'd send them to-day," he wrote on his card. "Didn't like the idea of my personal offering nailed to the club wall."

About nine o'clock I put on my silk dressing gown and went down to the library for the book about the girl who always had her hand in the man's coat pocket. I had got clear in when I saw Henry's red head over the top of a deep chair.

"Come in!" he called. "I was told there was no one at home, but methinks I know the step and the rustle."

"Don't look round," I said sharply. "I'm not dressed."

"Can't you stay a few minutes?"

"Certainly not."

"If I don't look?"

Well, it seemed silly to run. I was more covered up than I'd been the night before in my ball gown. Besides, it had occurred to me that Henry could be useful if he would. A sort of plan had popped into my head. Inspiration, I called it then.

"Pretty nice last night, wasn't it?" he asked, talking to the fireplace. "You looked some person, Kit, believe me."

"Considering that I've spent nineteen years getting ready, it should have gone off rather well."

"I suppose I'll never see you any more."

"This looks like it! Why?"

"You'll be so popular."

"Oh, that! I'm not sure, Henry. I'm not beautiful."

He jumped at that, and almost turned round.

"Not beautiful!" he said. "You're—you're the loveliest thing that ever lived, and you know it."

It began to look to me as if he wouldn't help after all. There was a sort of huskiness in his voice, a—

Oh, well, you know. I began on the plan, however.

"You'll see me, all right," I said. "I'll have other friends, of course. I hope so anyhow. But when one thinks who and what they are——"

"Good gracious, Kit! What are you driving at?"

"I'm young," I said. "I know that. But I'm not ignorant. And a really nice girl with ideals——"

"I'll have to get up," he said suddenly. "I'll stand with my back to you, if you insist, but I'll have to get up. What's all this about ideals?"

"You know very well," I put in with dignity. "If every time I meet a nice man people come to me with stories about him, or mother and father warn me against him, what am I to do?"

"Can't you stand behind a chair and let me face you? This is serious."

"Oh, turn round," I said recklessly. "If I hear any one coming I can run. Anyhow, it may be unconventional but I'm fully clothed."

"Are you being warned against me?" he threw at me like a bomb. "Because, if—if you are, it's absurd nonsense. I'm no saint, and I'd never be fit for you to— What silly story have you heard, Kit?"

He was quite white, and his red hair looked like a conflagration.

"It's not about you at all; it's about Russell Hill."

It took him a moment to breathe normally again.

"Oh—Russell!" he said. "Well, that's probably nonsense too. You don't mean to say your people object to your knowing Russell?"

"Not quite that," I said. "But I can't have him here, or go round with him, or anything of that sort."

"Do they venture to give a reason?"

"Toots Warrington."

It's queer about men, the way they stand up for each other. Henry knew as well as he knew anything that most of the girls we both knew were crazy about Russell. And if he cared for me—and the way he acted made me suspicious—he had a good chance to throw Russell into the discard that night. But he didn't. I knew well enough he wouldn't.

"That's perfect idiocy," he said sternly. "Society is organised along certain lines, and maybe if you and I had anything to do with it we'd change things. But there is no commandment or social law or anything else against a man having a married woman for a friend."

"Friend!"

"Exactly—friend."

"I don't care to have anything to do with him."

"You needn't, of course. But you owe it to Russell to give him a chance to set things straight. Anyhow he and Mrs. Warrington are not seeing each other much any more. It's off."

"The very fact that you say it is 'off' shows that it was once 'on.' "

He waved his hands in perfect despair. If I'd rehearsed him he couldn't have picked up his cues any better.

"I'm going to tell him," he said. "It's ridiculous. It's—it's libellous."

"I don't want him coming here explaining. I am not even interested."

"You're a perfect child, a stubborn child! Your mind's in pigtails, like your hair."

Yes, my hair was down. I have rather nice hair.

"If he comes here," I said with my eyes wide, "he will have to come when mother and father are out."

"I'll bring him," said Henry valiantly. "I'm not going to see him calumniated, that's all." Then something struck his sense of humour and he chuckled. "It will be a new and valuable experience to him," he said, "to have to come clandestinely. Do him good!"

I went upstairs then. It had been a fair day's work.

But it's hard to count on a family. Mother sprained her ankle getting out of the car that night and was laid up for three days. I chafed at first.

Henry might change his mind or one of the eleven get in some fine work. We declined everything that week, and I made some experiments with my hair and the aid of mother's maid. I wanted a sort of awfully feminine method—not sappy but not at all sophisticated. Toots Warrington is always waved and netted, and all the girls by that time had got earrings and were going round waved and netted too.

I wanted to fix my hair like a girl who slips her hand into a man's coat pocket because she can't help it, and then tries to get it out, and can't because his hand has got hold of it.

Then one night I got it. Henry had dropped in, and found mother with her foot up and the look of a dyspeptic martyr on her face, and father with a cold and a thermometer in his mouth.

"I've come to take Kit to the movies," he announced calmly. "Far be it from me not to contribute to the entertainment of a young lady who is just out!"

"Full of gerbs!" father grunted, referring to the movies of course, not me. But mother agreed.

"Do take her out, Henry," she said. "She's been on my nerves all evening."

So we went, and there was a girl in one of the pictures who had exactly the right hair arrangement. She had it loose and wavy about her face, and it blew about the way things do blow in the movies, and in the back it was a sort of soft wad.

It shows the association of ideas that I found my hand in Henry's coat pocket, and he grabbed it like a lunatic.

"You darling!" he said thickly. "Don't do that unless you mean it. I can't stand it."

I had to be very cool on the way home in the motor or he would have kissed me.

Mother and I went to a reception on the following Tuesday, and I wondered if mother noticed. She did. Coming home in the motor she turned and stared at me.

"Thank heaven, Kit," she said, "you still look like a young girl. All at once Ellie and the others look like married women. Earrings! It's absurd. And such earrings! I am quite sure," she went on, eying me, "that some of them had been smoking. I got an unmistakable whiff of it when I was talking with Bessie Willing."

Well, I had rinsed my mouth with mouth wash and dabbed my lips with cologne, so she got nothing from me. But I tasted like a drug store.

I am not smoking now. I am not doing much of anything. I—but I'm coming to that.

I'm no hypocrite. I'd been raised for one purpose, and that was to marry well. If I did it in my own way, and you think my way not exactly ethical,

I can't help it. This thing of sitting back and letting somebody find you and propose to you is ridiculous. There is only one life, and we have to make
the best we can of it.

Ethical! Don't girls always have the worst of
it anyhow? They can't go and ask the man. They
have to lie in wait and plan and scheme, or get left
and have their younger sisters come out and crowd
them, and at twenty-five or so begin to regard any
man at all as a prospect. Maybe my methods sound
a bit crude, but compared with the average girl I
know, I was delicate. I didn't play up my attrac-
tions, at least not more than was necessary. I was
using my mind, not my body.

III

On Tuesday night I was going to a dance. Mother
and father were dining out and were to meet me
later, so I was free until ten o'clock. That night
Henry brought Russell Hill.

I kept them waiting a few minutes, and came
down ready for the car. At the last minute I pulled
my hair a bit loose over my face, and the effect was
exactly right.

Henry was horribly uncomfortable, and left in
a few minutes. He was going with some people to
the dance, and would see us later. About all he
said was with his usual tact.

"You two ought to get together," he said. "There's a lot too much being whispered these days, and not enough talking out loud."

With that he went, and we two were left facing each other.

"This is one of Henry's inspirations, Miss Katherine," Russell said. "I—I don't usually have to wait until the family is out before I make a call."

"Families are queer," I said non-committally. There was a window open and I stood near it, under a pink lamp, and let my hair blow about.

"Are we going to sit down, or am I to be banished as soon as I've explained that I am a safe companion for a débutante?"

He was plainly laughing at me, although he was uncomfortable too. And I have some spirit left.

"I am afraid you are giving me credit for too much interest," I said. "This is Henry's idea, you know. You needn't defend yourself to me. You look—entirely safe."

He hated that. No man likes to look entirely safe. He put his hands in his pockets and half closed his eyes.

"Humph!" he said. "Then I gather that this whole meeting is a mistake. I'm respectable enough to be uninteresting, and the ban your people have placed on me doesn't particularly concern you!"

"That's not quite true," I said slowly. "I—if I

ever got a chance to know you really well, I'm sure we'd be—but I'll never get a chance, you know."

"Upon my word," he broke out, "I'd like to know just what your people have heard! But that doesn't matter. What really matters"—he had hardly taken his eyes off me—"what really matters is that I am going to see you again. Often!"

"It's impossible."

"Rot! We're always going to the same places. Am I absolutely warned off?"

"You're not. But I am."

He began to walk up and down the room. Half an hour before he had never given me a thought. Henry, I knew, had lugged him there by sheer force and a misplaced sense of justice. And now he was pacing about in a rage!

He stopped rather near me.

"If it's Mrs. Warrington all the fuss is about, it's imbecile," he said. "In the first place, there never was anything to it. In the second place, it's all over anyhow."

"I don't know what the fuss is about."

"You know the whole thing. Don't pretend you don't. You've got the face of a little saint, with all that fluffy hair, but your eyes don't belong to the rest, young lady. Are you going to dance with me to-night?"

"I'm afraid not."

"Well, you'll give me a little time, won't you? I suppose we can sit in a closet and talk, or hide on a veranda."

"It's—it's rather sneaking, isn't it?"

"That doesn't hurt it any for me."

So I promised, and, the car being announced, he put my wrap round my shoulders.

"Stunning hair you've got," he said from behind me. "Thank heaven for hair that isn't marceled and glued up in a net!"

I held out my hand in the hall, and he took it.

"I'm not such a bad lot after all, am I?" he demanded.

With my best spontaneous gesture I put my free hand over his as it held mine.

"I'm so sorry, so terribly sorry, if I've misunderstood," I said earnestly.

Wallace had gone to the outer door. Russell Hill stooped over and kissed my hand.

Well, it was working. An hour before I was one of what I'd heard he had called "the dolly dozen." Now, by merely letting him understand that he couldn't have what he'd never wanted, he was eager.

We sat out one dance under the stairs, and an intermission in a pantry while the musicians who had been stationed there were getting their supper. He tried to hold my hand and I drew it away—not too fast, but so he could understand the struggle I was having between duty and inclination. And we talked about love.

I said I liked to play round with men and have a good time and all that sort of thing, but that I thought I was naturally cold.

"You cold?" he said. "It's only that the right man has not come along."

"I've known a good many. A good many have— have——"

"Cared for you? Of course. They're not fools or blind. Look here, I'm going to ring you up now and then."

"I think you'd better not."

"If I'm not to see you and not to telephone, how's this friendship of ours to get on?"

"People who are real friends don't need to see each other."

"That's the first real débutante speech you've made to-night. Now, see here, I'm going to see you again, and often. And I'm going to ring you up. What's your tailor's name?"

I told him, and he put it down on his dance card.

"All right," he said. "Herschenrother is now my middle name, and if it's not convenient to talk, you can give me the high sign."

Toots Warrington came along just then with an army officer she'd taken on. They got clear round the palms and into the pantry before they saw us, and her face was funny.

Mother and I had another heart-to-heart talk that night on the way home. Father had gone a couple of hours earlier and we had the car to ourselves. Mother was tired and irritable.

"It seemed to me, Kit," she observed, "that you danced with every hopeless ineligible there. You danced three times with Henry."

"For heaven's sake, mother," I snapped, "let poor Henry alone. Henry is the most useful person I know."

"You can't play with red-headed people and not get burned," mother said with unconscious humour. "He's very fond of you, Kit. I watched him to-night."

"The fonder the better," I said flippantly. Yes, that's what I said. When I look back on that evening and think how little Henry entered into my plans, and the rest of it, it makes me cold.

"I want you to do one thing—just one, mother: I want you to be very cool to Russell Hill."

"Cool!"

"And I want you to forbid me to see him."

"I'm not insane, Katherine."

"Listen, mother," I said desperately. "All his life Russell Hill has had everything he wanted. He's had so much that—that he's got a sort of social indigestion. The only things he wants now are the things he can't have. So he can't have me."

Mother's not very subtle. And she was alarmed. I can still see her trying to readjust her ideas, and getting tied up in them, and coming a mental cropper, so to speak.

"If he can't have me he'll want me."

"I'm not sure of it. He——"

"Mother," I said in despair, "you've been married for twenty years, and you know less about men in a month than I do in a minute. Please forbid him the house—not in so many words, but act it."

"Why?" she said feebly.

"Anything you can think of—Toots Warrington will do."

She got out her salts and held them to her nose.

"I feel as though I'm losing my mind," she said at last. "But if you're set on it——"

That was all until we got home. Then on the stairs I thought of something.

"Oh, yes," I said. "No matter what I am doing, mother, if Herschenrother the tailor calls up I want to go to the telephone."

I can still see her staring after me with her mouth open as I went up the stairs.

Herschenrother called me up the next morning, and asked me how I was, and how the dragons were, and if there was any chance of my walking in the park at five o'clock. I said there was, and called up Henry and asked him to walk with me.

"I should say so," he said. "You've only got to ask me, Kit. I'm always ready to hang round."

There was rather a bad half hour in the park, and for a time I felt that Henry had been a wrong move. But, as it turned out he hadn't, for Russell took advantage of somebody's signalling to Henry from a machine to say:

"Just a bit afraid of me still, aren't you?"

"Why?"

"You brought Henry. I know the signs. You asked him, and he's so set up about it that he's walking on clouds."

"I am afraid."

"Of me?"

"Of myself."

He caught my arm as he helped me across a puddle, and squeezed it.

"Good girl!" he said.

And later on, when Henry was called again— he's terribly popular, Henry is—he had another chance.

"I'm going to see you alone if I have to steal you," he said.

Herschenrother called up again the next day, and Madge, who had come home for the Christmas holidays, called me.

"Gee, Kit," she said, "you must be getting a trousseau. That tailor's always on the phone."

I went.

"Hello," said Russell's voice, "how about that fitting?"

"I don't know. I'm horribly busy to-day."

"It's very important. I—I can't go ahead without it."

"Oh, all right," I said. Madge was listening and I had to be careful. "I must have the suit."

"You can have anything I've got. How about the Art Gallery? Art is long and time is fleeting. Nobody goes there."

"Very well, four o'clock," I replied, and rang off.

"Rather a nice voice," Madge said, eying me. "Think I'll go along, Kit. I've been shut up in school until the mere thought of even a good-looking tailor makes me thrill."

She was so insistent that I had to go to mother finally, and mother told her she would have to practise. She was furious. Really, mother turned out to be a most understanding person. I got to be quite fond of her. We had a chat that afternoon that brought us closer together than ever.

"Things are doing pretty well, mother," I said when she'd finished Madge.

"He must be interested when he would take that absurd name."

"And the Art Gallery! I dare say he has never voluntarily been inside of one in his life."

"Kit," mother said, "what about your father?"

"Haven't you told him?"

"No; he wouldn't understand."

Of course not. I knew men well enough for that. They believe that life and marriage arrange themselves. That it's all a sort of combination of Providence and chance. Predestination plus opportunity!

"Can't you tell him you've heard something about Russell, and that he'd better be cool to him?"

"And have him turn the man down if it really comes to a proposal!"

"That won't matter," I told her. "We'll probably elope anyhow."

Mother opposed that vigorously. She said that no matter how good a match it was, there was always something queer about an elopement. And anyhow she'd been giving wedding gifts for years and it was time something came in instead of going out. It was the only point we differed on.

Well, father did his best to queer things that very day. All the way through I played in hard luck. Just when things were going right something happened.

I met Russell at the Art Gallery. It was a cold day, but I left my muff at home. It was about time for the coat-pocket business. I couldn't afford to wait, for one or two of the girls were wearing their hair like mine, and I'd heard that Toots Warrington had gone to Russell and asked him how he liked kindergartening. Bessie Willing, who told me, said that Russell's reply was:

"It's rather pleasant. I'm reversing things. Instead of going from the cradle to the grave, I'm going from the grave to the cradle."

I don't believe he said it. In the first place, he is too polite. In the second place, he is too stupid. But as Toots is not young he may have thought of it.

He was waiting near a heater, and we sat down together. I shivered.

"Cold, honey?" he asked.

"Hands are cold. Do you mind if I put one in your coat pocket?"

Did he mind? He did not. He was very polite at first and emptied the pocket of various things, including a letter which he mentioned casually was a bill. But after a moment he slid his hand in on top of mine.

"You're a wonderful young person," he said, "and you've got me going."

Then he squeezed the hand until it hurt. Suddenly he looked up.

"Great Scott!" he said. "There's Henry!"

Of course it was Henry. He had brought a cata-

logue and was going painstakingly from one picture
to another. He did not see us at first, and we had
time to stand up and be looking at a landscape when
he got to us. He looked moderately surprised and
waited to mark something in the catalogue before
he joined us.

"Bully show, isn't it?" he said cheerfully. "Never
saw so many good 'uns. Well, what are you children up to?"

"Dropped in to get warm," said Russell. And
I was going to add something, but Henry's interest
in us had passed evidently. He marked another
cross in the catalogue and went on, with the light
shining on his red hair and his soul clearly as up-
lifted as his chin.

"You needn't worry about Henry," I said. "He's
a friend of the family, and I'll just call him up and
tell him not to say anything."

"I used to think he was fond of you."

"That's all over," I said casually. "It was just
one of the things that comes and goes. Like this
little—acquaintance of ours."

"What do you mean, goes?" he demanded almost
fiercely.

"They always do, don't they? Awfully pleasant
things don't last. And we can't go on meeting in-
definitely. Some one will tell father, and then where
will I be?"

That was a wrong move about father.

"That reminds me," he said. "Are you sure your father dislikes me such a lot?"

"Don't let's talk about it," I said, and closed my eyes.

"Because I met him to-day, and he nearly fell on my neck and hugged me."

Can you beat that? I was stunned.

"The more he detests people," I managed finally, "the more polite he is."

Then I took off my gloves and fell to rubbing the fingers of my left hand. And he moved round and put it in the other coat pocket without a word, with his hand over it, and the danger was past, for the time anyhow.

Mother came round that evening about the elopement.

"Perhaps you are right, Katherine," she said. "A lot of people will send things when the announcement cards go out. And Russell can afford to buy you anything you want anyhow."

Madge was a nuisance all that week. She was always at the telephone first when it rang, and I did not like her tone when she said it was Herschenrother again. Once I could have sworn that I saw her following me, but she ducked into a shop when I turned round.

She had transferred her affections to Henry, and

he took her to a cotillon or two for the school set, and played round with the youngsters generally, and showed her a sweet time, as she said.

But once when mother and I had been shut in my room, going over my clothes and making notes of what I would take with me, if the thing came to an elopement—I was pretty sure by that time, and we planned a sort of week-end outfit without riding things—I opened the door suddenly, and Madge was just outside.

Well, we got her back to school finally, and Henry took her to the train. I remember mother's watching them as they got into the car together.

"That wouldn't be so bad for Madge," she said reflectively. "She is bound to marry badly anyhow, she's so impulsive, and Henry would be a good counterweight. He is very dependable."

"She would make him most unhappy," I said. "Probably Henry would be all right for Madge, but how about Madge for Henry?"

Mother looked at me and said nothing.

Russell proposed at the end of the next week, and I refused. He proposed in a movie. We'd had to give up the Art Gallery because Henry was always taking people through it. He took Toots one afternoon, and that finished us.

There was a little talk that Henry and Toots were getting rather thick. The army man's leave was up, and she had to have somebody. There was probably something to it. We saw them in the park one afternoon sitting on a bench, and I could have sworn she had her hand in his coat pocket!

Well, I refused Russell.

"Why?" he said. "You're crazy about me, and you know it."

"I'm not going to marry a past," I said. "You'd make me horribly unhappy."

"I'd never bore you, that's one thing."

"No, but you might find me dull."

"Dull! Darling girl, I've never had as interesting a month in my life."

I said nothing. After a minute:

"Do you remember the first night we really met?"

"In the pantry. Yes."

"Do you remember what you said about being cold? And I told you it was a question of the right man?"

I remembered.

"Well, I'm the man," he said triumphantly. "Don't fool yourself—that little hand of yours slips into my coat pocket as if it belonged there. And it does."

He pulled it out and kissed it. Luckily the theatre was dark.

Two days later I consented to elope with him.

Mother was quite delirious when I told her. She came over and kissed my cheek.

"You've never disappointed me, Kit, never," she said. "If only Madge would do as well."

She sighed.

"Madge will probably marry for love, and be happy," I snapped. It was a silly speech. I haven't an idea why I made it.

"And shabby," said mother.

I turned on her sharply. The strain of the last month was over, and I dare say I went to pieces.

"It's all very well for you to be satisfied," I cried. "You're not going to marry Russell Hill, and have him call you 'girlie,' and see his hat move every time he raises his eyebrows. I am."

She went out very stiffly, and sent her maid in with hot tea.

I was out at a theatre party that night, and mother was in my room when I got back.

"I want to talk to you, Katherine," she said, "I've been uneasy all evening."

"If you mean about what I said this afternoon, please forget it, mother. I was tired and nervous. I didn't mean it."

"Not that. I don't want any mistake about this elopement. Now and then those things have a way of going wrong. Quite often there is trouble about a license or a minister."

"Send father ahead," I said flippantly.

"Not father. But some one really ought to look after things. Russell is not the sort to arrange anything in advance. I thought perhaps Henry—"

"Henry!"

"He is reliable," said mother. "And he has your well-being at heart. He is more like a brother than a good many brothers I know."

I could scream my head off when I think of it now. For we fixed on Henry, and I telephoned him to come round to dinner. He seemed rather surprised when he heard my voice.

"Honestly, Kit," he said, "do you want me?"

"I want you to do something for me."

"Then I'll come. That's all that's necessary."

But it wasn't as easy as it had promised after all. There's something so downright about Henry. He was standing in front of the library fire after dinner when I told him.

"Henry," I said, "I am going to be married."

He did not say anything at first. Then:

"Well?" he asked.

"Do you know to whom?"

"Yes."

"Aren't you going to say anything?"

"I don't know what I can say," he said very slowly and carefully. "If each of you cares a lot, that's all there is to it, isn't it? The point is, of

course, why you are doing it. If it's to cut out somebody else, or to get money or anything like that, I'm
not going to wish you happiness, because you won't
deserve it. If you're in love with him, that's different."

Did you ever try to tell a lie to a red-headed young
man with blue eyes? It's extremely difficult.

"I'm not in love with him, Henry," I said. I
was astounded to hear myself saying it.

"Then you're giving him a crooked deal."

"He's not in love with me either. So that's
even."

"Then why——"

"Because he thinks he can't have me," I said.
"I'm marrying him because he's the most marriageable man I know, and I have to marry money. I've
been raised for that. And he's marrying me because
I'm the only girl whose people didn't fling her at
him."

"Then I wish you joy of each other!" he said
hoarsely, and slammed out of the room and out of
the house.

I haven't the faintest idea what came over me
that night. I went upstairs and cried my eyes out.

A few days later, after a round of luncheons, dinners and dances until I was half dead, I had a free
evening. The elopement had been set for Friday,
and it was Wednesday. Mother and father were

out, and I went downstairs for a book. I had got
it and was just going out when I saw Henry's red
head over the back of the leather chair by the fire.

I went over. He was not reading. He was just
sitting, his long legs stretched out in front of him.

"Hello, Kit," he said calmly. "I knew this was
an off night. Sit down."

I sat down, rather suspicious of his manner.
Henry can't dissemble.

"About the other night," he said, "I was taken by
surprise. Just forget it, Kit. Now, when are you
going to pull this thing off?"

I told him, and where.

"Russell made any arrangements?"

"I haven't asked."

"Probably not. He'll expect to get out of the
train and find a license and a preacher on the platform. I'd better be best man, and go down there
a day before to fix things."

Well, it wasn't flattering to see him so eager to
get me married. There had been a time when I
thought— However—

"Oh!" I said.

"Better do it right while you're about it," he
said. "You might give me one of your rings, and
I'll order a wedding ring. Platinum or gold?"

"Platinum," I said feebly.

"Anything inside?"

"The—the date, I suppose."

"No initials or anything like that?"

I roused from a sort of stupor of astonishment.

"I like a very narrow ring," I said. "There won't be room for much inside. The date will do. But I'm sure that Russell——"

"All right if he does. Perhaps I'd better not put in the date. Then, if he takes one along, I can return this and have it credited to him."

"You're very thoughtful."

"Not at all," he said with the first atom of feeling he'd shown. "I don't approve of anything about this business; but if it's going to happen, it's going to happen right!"

He got up and stood in front of the fire.

"The thing to be sure of, Kit," he said soberly, "is that you don't love any one else. It's bad enough as it is, but that would be worse."

"I wouldn't dare to be in love with any one who wasn't eligible," I said, not looking at him. "I've been raised for just what I'm doing. I'm fulfilling my destiny."

"There's nobody else, then?"

"Who could there be?"

"That's twice I've asked you a perfectly simple question, Kit, and you have evaded it. The plain truth, of course, is that you are in love, absolutely single-heartedly in love, but not with Russell."

"Then who?" I demanded sharply.

"With yourself," he said, and picked up his hat and went out.

IV

Russell and I eloped on a Friday morning. Mother and I packed my dressing case and a bag, and I gave her an itemized list of what was to be sent on in my trunk when I wired for it. She was greatly relieved to know that Henry was looking after things, especially the ring.

"I do hope he gets a narrow one," she said. "Wedding rings are nonsense at any time. You can never wear other rings with them. But if it is platinum you can have it set with diamonds later on."

I think she was disappointed when I refused to leave a note on my dressing table for her.

"That's out of date, mother," I said. "You needn't know anything until you get my wire that it's over. Then you can call up the newspapers and deny it. That's the best way to let them know."

Then she went out, per agreement, after kissing me good-by, and I called a taxicab and eloped.

Did you ever have a day when things went wrong with you and when you knew that the fault was somewhere in you? Well, that was that sort of day.

The minute I was in the taxicab I was uncomfortable. All at once I didn't want to be married. I hoped Russell would miss the train, and I could go back home and be a spinster lady and be on committees.

But he did not miss the train. He was there, waiting. He had on a very ugly necktie and an English ulster that made his chest dish in, although he has a good figure.

"Hello, girlie," he said. "Stuff all here? Any excitement at home? No? Nice work."

My lips felt stiff.

"Train's waiting," he said. "What do you think of Henry? Big lift, that is. I've never been married before. I'm fairly twittering."

We got into the train. There was no Pullman. Not that it mattered, but it helped to upset me. I hated eloping in a day coach. And a woman with a market basket sat across the aisle, and the legs of a chicken stuck out.

Russell squeezed into the seat beside me.

"Jove, this is great!" he said. "Aren't you going to put your hand in my coat pocket, honey?"

Quite suddenly I said:

"I don't want to."

He drew away a trifle.

"You're nervous," he said. "So am I, for that matter. D'you mind if I go and smoke?"

I didn't mind. I thought if I had to see that ulster dishing in and that tie another minute I'd go crazy.

I grew calmer when he had gone. Here was the thing I had worked so hard for, mine at last. I thought of Toots, and her face when she saw the papers. I thought of Ellie Clavering and Bessie Willing and Margaret North and the others, with their earrings and the imitation of Toots and all the rest of it. I felt rather better. When Russell came back I could even smile at him.

"I wish I could have a cigarette," I said.

He turned and put a hand over mine.

"You're going to cut that out, you know, girlie," he said. "I can't have my wife smoking."

Yes, that's what he said. For ten years he'd sent girls cigarettes and offered them cigarettes and sat with them in corners while they smoked cigarettes. But he didn't want his wife smoking. Wasn't it typical?

Oh, well, I didn't care. I'd do as I liked once we were married. Then about half way, without the slightest warning, I knew I couldn't marry him. Marry him! Why, I didn't even like him. And the way he made me sit with my hand in his coat pocket was sickening.

"I don't think I'll marry you after all," I said.

"Eh? What?"

"I said I've changed my mind. I won't do it."

"I haven't changed mine."

"I'm not really in love with you."

"You're nervous," he said calmly. "Go ahead and talk. It's the new psychology. Never bury your worries. Talk 'em out and get rid of 'em."

"I was never forbidden to see you."

"All right," he said contentedly. "I knew that all along. What else?"

"Even my hand in your coat pocket is a trick."

"Sure it is, but it's a nice trick. What else?"

"I'm not going to marry you."

"Oh, yes, you are. You can't very well go back, can you? Mother's probably called up the papers already."

Then he sat up and looked at me.

"Now, look here, young lady," he said. "I'm no idiot. I knew before you were born some of the stunts you pulled. I've never been fooled for a minute about them. But you're going to marry me. Why? Because I'm crazy about you. That's why. And that's enough."

It was terrible. And there was no way out, none. The train rumbled on. There was a tunnel and he kissed me. It was a short tunnel.

Somebody behind chuckled.

And then at last it was over, and we were there, and I was being led like a sheep to the altar, and

Henry was on the platform with ring and license and all the implements of sacrifice.

"Behold," said Russell from the train platform, "the family friend is on hand. Whose idea was Henry, anyhow? His or yours or mother's?"

Henry came up. He looked cheerful enough, although I fancied he was pale. I liked his necktie. I always liked Henry's ties.

"Hello," he said. "Everything here? Where's your luggage?"

"Baggage car," said Russell. "Look after Kit, Henry, will you? I'll see to it."

He hadn't taken two steps before Henry had clutched my arm.

"I knew you wouldn't," he said. "I can see it in your face."

"Henry!" I gasped. "What am I to do?"

"You're to marry me," he said in a sort of fierce whisper. "Don't stop to argue. I've always meant to marry you. Quick, into the taxi!"

That's all I remember just then, except hearing him say he had the license and the ring, and an uproar from where we'd left Russell and all his money on the platform.

"Wha-what sort of license?" I asked, with my teeth chattering from pure fright. "If it's in Russell's name it's not good, is it?"

"It's in my name," said Henry, grimly.

"But the ring—that's Russell's."

"Not at all," said Henry, still without an atom of tenderness. "I bought it and paid for it. It's got 'From H. to K.' inside of it. Very small," he added hastily. "It's quite narrow, as you requested."

"Henry," I said, sitting up stiffly, "what would I have done if you hadn't been round?"

"You needn't worry about that. After this I'll always be round. I don't intend to be underfoot," he volunteered, "but I'll be within call. As a matter of fact," he added, "I've been within call practically all of the last month. It's taken a lot of time."

If only he had said something agreeable or yielding, or looked anything but grim and efficient, I could have stood it. But, there we were, on our way to be married, and he looked as sentimental as a piano tuner.

All at once it came over me that it was Henry, it always had been Henry, it always would be Henry. And he looked calm and altruistic and rather hollow round his eyes.

"If you're only doing this to save me," I said, "you needn't, you know. I can go home, even if the papers have got it."

"Don't make me any more nervous than I am, Kit," he said. "I'm about evenly divided as to beating you up or kissing you. Any extra strain, and it's one or the other."

"Don't beat me, Henry."

"I'm damnably poor, Kit," he said.

For reply I slid my hand into his coat pocket. He melted quite suddenly after that, and put his arms round me. I knew I was being a fool but I was idiotically happy.

"Henry," I said, "do you know that verse in the Bible, that as a partridge sits on eggs and fails to hatch them, so too the person who gets riches without deserving them?"

He held me off and looked at me as if he suspected my sanity. Then he kissed me.

V

Mother has never really forgiven me. It put her in so awfully wrong, of course. For she called up the newspapers, and said that if they received a report that I had eloped with Mr. Russell Hill, they were please to deny it.

Of course they sent reporters everywhere at once. And they traced me to the station. About the time mother was reading the headlines "Society Bud and Well-Known Clubman Elope," and wiring Madge, she got Henry's telegram.

She thinks I threw away the chance of a lifetime.

But since the day before yesterday I've been wondering. I was going over Henry's old suits, getting them ready to be cleaned and pressed. We have to be very economical. And in a pocket I came across this letter:

"DEAR BOY: We have decided on the eleven-o'clock train. For the love of Mike don't miss meeting it! And after thinking it over carefully, you're right. When I go to see after the luggage will be the best time. Yours,

"RUSSELL."

CLARA'S LITTLE ESCAPADE

CLARA'S LITTLE ESCAPADE

"THE plain truth is," said Carrie Smith, "that, no matter how happy two people may be together, the time comes when they are bored to death with each other."

Nobody said anything. It was true and we knew it. Ida Elliott put down the scarf she was knitting for the Belgians and looked down over the hill to where a lot of husbands were playing in the swimming pool.

"It isn't just a matter of being bored, you know, Carrie," she said. "A good many of us have made mistakes." Then she sighed. Ida is not really unhappy, but she likes to think she is.

None of the rest made any comment. But one or two of the other girls put down their knitting and looked out over the hills.

"I hope you don't mind my saying it, Clara," Carrie said, turning to me; "but it's a mistake to have a week-end party like this. Last night when I played pool with your Bill after the rest of you had gone upstairs, Wallie refused to speak to me when I went to bed. He's still sulking."

I am not sensitive; but when they everyone turned

on me and said it was a beautiful party, but why, in heaven's name, had I asked only husbands and not one extra man, it made me a trifle hot.

"As most of us see our husbands only during week-ends," I said tartly, "I should think this sort of family reunion would be good for us."

Carrie sniffed.

"See them!" she snapped. "They've been a part of the landscape since we came, and that's all. Either they're in the pool, or playing clock golf, or making caricatures of themselves on the tennis court. A good photograph would be as comforting, and wouldn't sulk."

Well, the whole thing really started from that. I made up my mind, somehow or other, to even up with them. I'd planned a really nice party, and even if they were bored they might have had the politeness to conceal it.

Even now, badly as things turned out, I maintain that the idea was a good one. I had a bad time, I'll admit that. But the rest of them were pretty unhappy for a while. The only thing I can't quite forgive is that Bill—but that comes later on.

There had been very little doing all spring. Everybody was poor, and laying up extra motors, and trying to side-step appeals for Eastern relief, and hiding dressmakers' bills. There were hardly any dividends at all, and what with the styles completely changing from wide skirts to narrow ones, so that not a thing from last year would do, and the men talking nothing but retrenchment and staying at the table hours after every dinner party, fighting the war over again, while we sat and knitted, I never remember a drearier spring.

"Although," Carrie Smith said with truth, "the knitting's rather good for us. No woman can enjoy a cigarette and knit at the same time."

The craze for dancing was dying away, too, and nothing came along to take its place. The débutantes were playing tennis, but no woman over twenty-two should ever play tennis, so most of us were out of that. Anyhow it's violent. And bridge, for anything worth while, was apt to be too expensive.

But to go back.

We sat and knitted and yawned, and the husbands put on dressing gowns and ambled up the hill and round to the shower baths in the basement. I looked at Bill. Bill is my husband and I'm fond of Bill. But there are times when he gets on my nerves. He has a faded old bathrobe that saw him through college and his honeymoon, and that he still refuses to part with, and he had it on.

It was rather short, and Bill's legs, though serviceable, are not beautiful.

He waved his hand to me.

"If you'd do a little of that sort of thing, Clara,"

he called, "you wouldn't need to have the fat rubbed
off you by an expensive masseuse."

"Quite a typical husbandly speech!" said Carrie
Smith.

"Do they ever think of anything but exercise and
expense?"

Well, the men bathed and dressed and had whisky-
and-sodas, and came out patronisingly and joined us
at tea on the terrace. But inside of ten minutes they
were in a group round the ball news and the financial
page of the evening papers, and we were alone again.

Carrie Smith came over and sat down beside me,
with her eyes narrowed to a slit.

"I didn't want to hurt your feelings, Clara," she
said, "but you see what I mean. They're not interested in us. We manage their houses and bring up
their children. That's all."

As Carrie was the only one who had any children, and as they were being reared by a trained
nurse and a governess, and the baby yelled like an
Apache if Carrie went near him, her air of virtue
was rather out of place. However:

"What would you recommend?" I asked wearily.
"They're all alike, aren't they?"

"Not all." Her eyes were still narrowed. And
at that moment Wallie Smith came over and threw
an envelope into her lap.

"It came to the office by mistake," he said grimly.

"What made you have your necklace reset when I'm practically bankrupt?"

"I bought hardly any new stones," she flashed at him. "Anyhow, I intend to be decently clothed. Tear it up; nobody's paying any bills."

He stalked away, and Carrie looked at me.

"No," she said slowly, "they are not all alike. Thank heaven there are a few men who don't hoist the dollar mark as a flag. Clara, do you remember Harry Delaney?"

I looked at Carrie.

A little spot of red had come into each of her cheeks, and her eyes, mere slits by now, were fixed on the far-away hills.

She and Harry had been engaged years ago, and she threw him over because of his jealous nature. But she seemed to have forgotten that.

"Of course," I said, rather startled.

"He was a dear. Sometimes I think he was the most generous soul in the world. I cannot imagine his fussing about a necklace, or sulking for hours over a bit of innocent pleasure like my playing a game of pool after a lot of sleepyheads had gone to bed."

"What time did you and Bill go upstairs?"

"Something after two. We got tired of playing and sat out here and talked. I knew you wouldn't mind, Clara. You've got too much sense. Surely a woman ought to be allowed friends, even if she is married."

"Oh, friends!" I retorted. "If she's going to keep her husband a friend she's got her hands full. Certainly I'm not jealous of you and Bill, Carrie. But it's not friends most of us want, if you're after the truth. We want passionate but perfectly respectable, commandment-keeping lovers!"

Carrie laughed, but her colour died down.

"How silly you are!" she said, and got up. "Maybe we'd like to feel that we're not clear out of the game, but that's all. We're a little tired of being taken for granted. I don't want a lover; I want amusement, and if I'd married Harry Delaney I'd have had it."

"If you'd married him he would have been down there at the pool, showing off like a goldfish in a bowl, the same as the others."

"He would not. He can't swim," said Carrie, and sauntered away. Somehow I got the impression that she had been sounding me, and had got what she wanted. She looked very handsome that night, and wore the necklace. Someone commented on it at dinner, and Wallie glared across at it.

"It isn't paid for," he said, "and as far as I can see, it never will be."

Of course, even among old friends, that was going rather far.

Well, the usual thing happened after dinner. The men smoked and argued, and we sat on the terrace and yawned. When they did come out it was to say that golf and swimming had made them sleepy, and Jim Elliott went asleep in his chair. Carrie said very little, except once to lean over and ask me if I remembered the name of the man Alice Warrington had thrown over for Ted. When I told her she settled back into silence again.

The next morning all the husbands were up early and off to the club for a Sunday's golfing. At ten o'clock a note came in on my breakfast tray from Carrie.

"Slip on something and come to my room," it said.

When I got there Ida and Alice Warrington were there already, and Carrie was sitting up in bed, with the same spots of colour I'd seen before. I curled up on the bed with my hands round my knees.

"Go to it, Carrie," I said. "If it's church, it's too late. If it's a picnic, it looks like rain."

"Close the door, Ida," said Carrie. "Girls, I'm getting pretty tired of this."

"Of what?"

"Of dragging the matrimonial ball and chain wherever I go, and having to hear it clank and swear and sulk, and—all the rest. I'm tired, and so are all of you. Only I'm more honest."

"It's all rather a mess," Ida said languidly. "But divorce is a mess too. And, anyhow, what's the use of changing? Just as one gets to know a man's pet stories, and needn't pretend to laugh at them any more, why take on a new bunch of stories—or habits?"

"The truth is," said Carrie, ignoring her, "that they have all the good times. They don't have to look pretty. Their clothes last forever. And they're utterly selfish socially. You girls know how much they dance with the married women when there are any débutantes about."

We knew.

"The thing to do," said Carrie, "is to bring them back to a sense of obligation. They've got us. We stay put. They take us to parties and get up a table of bridge for us, and go off to a corner with a chit just out of school, or dance through three handkerchiefs and two collars, and grumble at paying our bridge losses. Or else they stay at home, and nothing short of a high explosive would get them out of their chairs."

"Destructive criticism," said Alice Warrington, "never gets anywhere. We agree with you. There's no discussion. Are you recommending the high explosive?"

"I am," said Carrie calmly. "I propose to wake them up, and to have a good time doing it."

Well, as it turned out, it was I who wakened them up, and nobody had a very good time about it.

"There's just one man a husband is always jealous of," Carrie went on, and her eyes were slitted as usual. "That's the man his wife could have married and didn't."

I expect I coloured, for Bill has always been insanely jealous of Roger Waite, although honestly I never really cared for Roger. We used to have good times together, of course. You know.

Carrie's plan came out by degrees.

"It will serve two purposes," she said. "It will bring the men to a sense of responsibility, and stop this silly nonsense about bills and all that sort of thing. And it will be rather fun. It's a sin to drop old friends. Does Wallie drop his? Not so you could notice it. Every time I'm out of town he lives at Grace Barnabee's."

Carrie had asked us all to spend the next weekend with her, but the husbands were going to New York for the polo game and she had called the party off. But now it was on again.

"Do you girls remember the house party I had when Wallie was in Cuba, before we were engaged? We had a gorgeous time. I'm going to repeat it. It's silly to say lightning doesn't strike twice in the same place. Of course it does, if one doesn't use lightning rods. Peter Arundel for Alice, and Roger

for you, Clara. Ida, you were in Europe, but we'll
let you in. Who'll you have?"

"Only one?" asked Ida.

"Only one."

Ida chose Wilbur Bayne, and Carrie wrote the
notes right there in bed, with a pillow for a desk,
and got ink on my best linen sheets.

"I'm sorry I never thought of it before," she said.
"The house party is bound to be fun, and if it turns
out well we'll do it regularly. I'll ask in a few
people for dancing Saturday night, but we'll keep
Sunday for ourselves. We'll have a deliciously sentimental day."

She sat back and threw out her arms.

"Good Lord," she said, "I'm just ripe for a bit
of sentiment. I want about forty-eight hours without bills or butlers or bridge. I'm going to send my
diamond necklace to a safe deposit, and get out my
débutante pearls, and have the wave washed out of
my hair, and fill in the necks of one or two gowns.
I warn you fairly, there won't be a cigarette for any
of you."

When I left them they were already talking
clothes, and Carrie had a hand glass and was looking at herself intently in it.

"I've changed, of course," she sighed. "One can't
have two children and not show the wear and tear

of maternity. I could take off five pounds by going on a milk diet. I think I will."

She went on the diet at luncheon that day, and Wallie told her that if she would cut out heavy dinners and wine her stomach would be her friend, not her enemy. She glanced at me, but I ignored her. Somehow I was feeling blue.

The week-end had not been a success, and the girls had not been slow to tell me about it. The very eagerness with which they planned for the next week told me what a failure I'd had. Even then the idea of getting even somehow with Carrie was in the back of my mind.

The men did some trap shooting that afternoon, and during dinner Jim started a discussion about putting women on a clothes allowance and making them keep within it.

"I can systematise my business," he said, "but I can't systematise my home. I'm spending more now than I'm getting out of the mill."

Wallie Smith came up to scratch about that time by saying that his mother raised him with the assistance of a nursemaid, and no governess and trained nurse nonsense.

"That is why I insist on a trained nurse and a governess," said Carrie coldly, and took another sip of milk.

They went home that night, and Bill, having seen them into the motors, came up on the terrace.

"Bully party, old dear," he said enthusiastically. "Have 'em often, won't you?"

He sat down near me and put a hand over mine. All at once I was sorry I'd accepted Carrie's invitation. Not that there would be any harm in seeing Roger again, but because Bill wouldn't like it. The touch of his warm hand on mine, the quiet of the early summer night after the noise that had gone before, the scent of the honeysuckle over the pergola, all combined to soften me.

"I'm glad you had a good time, Bill," I said after a little silence. "I'm afraid the girls didn't enjoy it much. You men were either golfing or swimming or shooting, and there wasn't much to do but talk."

Bill said nothing. I thought he might be resentful, and I was in a softened mood.

"I didn't really mind your staying downstairs the other night with Carrie," I said. "Bill, do smell the honeysuckle. Doesn't it remind you of the night you asked me to marry you?"

Still Bill said nothing. I leaned over and looked at him. As usual he was asleep.

About the middle of the week Roger Waite called me up. We did not often meet—two or three times in the winter at a ball, or once in a season at a dinner. Ida Elliott always said he avoided me because it hurt him to see me. We had been rather sentimental. He would dance once with me, saying very little, and go away as soon as he decently could directly the dance was over. Sometimes I had thought that it pleased him to fancy himself still in love with me, and it's perfectly true that he showed no signs of marrying. It was rather the thing for the débutantes to go crazy about Roger. He had an air of knowing such a lot and keeping it from them.

"Why don't you keep him around?" Ida asked me once. "He's so ornamental. I'm not strong for tame cats, but I wouldn't mind Roger on the hearthrug myself."

But up to this time I'd never really wanted anybody on the hearthrug but Bill. If I do say it, I was a perfectly contented wife until the time Carrie Smith made her historic effort to revive the past. "Let sleeping dogs lie" is my motto now—and tame cats too.

Well, Roger called me up, and there was the little thrill in his voice that I used to think he kept for me. I know better now.

"What's this about going out to Carrie Smith's?" he said over the phone.

"That's all," I replied. "You're invited and I'm going."

"O!" said Roger. And waited a moment. Then:

"I was going on to the polo," he said, "but of course—What's wrong with Bill and polo?"

"He's going."

"Oh!" said Roger. "Well, then, I think I'll go to Carrie's. It sounds too good to be true—you, and no scowling husband in the offing!"

"It's—it's rather a long time since you and I had a real talk."

"Too long," said Roger. "Too long by about three years."

That afternoon he sent me a great box of flowers. My conscience was troubling me rather, so I sent them down to the dinner table. Whatever happened I was not going to lie about them.

But Bill only frowned.

"I've just paid a florist's bill of two hundred dollars," he grumbled. "Cut out the American beauties, old dear."

It was not his tone that made me angry. It was his calm assumption that I had bought the things. As if no one would think of sending me flowers!

"If you would stop sending orchids to silly débutantes when they come out," I snapped, "there would be no such florist's bills."

One way or another Bill got on my nerves that week. He brought Wallie Smith home one night to dinner, and Wallie got on my nerves too. I could remember, when Wallie and Carrie were engaged and we were just married, how he used to come and talk us black in the face about Carrie.

"How's Carrie, Wallie?" I said during the soup.

"She's all right," he replied, and changed the subject. But later in the evening, while Bill was walking on the lawn with a cigar, he broke out for fair.

"Carrie's on a milk diet," he said apropos of nothing. "If she stays on it another week I'm going to Colorado. She's positively brutal, and she hasn't ordered a real dinner for anybody for a week."

"Really!" I said.

He got up and towered over me.

"Look here, Clara," he said; "you're a sensible woman. Am I fat? Am I bald? Am I a doddering and toothless venerable? To hear Carrie this past few days you'd think I need to wear overshoes when I go out in the grass."

I rather started, because I'd been looking at Bill at that minute and wondering if he was getting his feet wet. He had only pumps on.

"It isn't only that she's brutal," he said, "she has soft moments when she mothers me. Confound it, I don't want to be mothered! She's taken off eight pounds," he went on gloomily. "And that isn't the worst." He lowered his voice. "I found her crying over some old letters the other day. She isn't happy, Clara. You know she could have married a lot of fellows. She was the most popular girl I ever knew."

Well, I'd known Carrie longer than he had, and of course a lot of men used to hang round her house because there was always something to do. But I'd never known that such a lot of them made love to Carrie or wanted to marry her. She was clever enough to hesitate over Wallie, but, believe me, she knew she had him cinched before she ran any risk. However:

"I'm sure you've tried to make her happy," I said. "But of course she was awfully popular."

I'm not so very keen about Carrie, but the way I felt that week, when it was a question between a husband and a wife, I was for the wife. "Of course," I said as Bill came within hearing distance, "it's not easy, when one's had a lot of attention, to settle down to one man, especially if the man is considerably older and—and settled."

That was a wrong move, as it turned out. For Bill, who never says much, got quieter than ever, and announced, just before he went to bed, that he'd given up the polo game. I was furious. I'd had one or two simple little frocks run up for Carrie's party, and by the greatest sort of luck I'd happened on a piece of flowered lawn almost exactly like one Roger used to be crazy about.

For twenty-four hours things hung in the balance.

Bill has a hideous way of doing what he says he'll do. Roger had sent more flowers—not roses this time, but mignonette and valley lilies, with a few white orchids. It looked rather bridey. It would have been too maddening to have Bill queer the whole thing at the last minute.

But I fixed things at bridge one night by saying that I thought married people were always better off for short separations, and that I was never so fond of Bill as when he'd been away for a few days.

"Polo for me!" said Bill.

And I went out during my dummy hand and telephoned Carrie.

I hope I have been clear about the way the thing began. I feel that my situation should be explained. For one thing, all sorts of silly stories are going round, and it is stupid of people to think they cannot ask Roger and me to the same dinners. If Bill would only act like a Christian, and not roar the moment his name is mentioned, there would be a chance for the thing to die out. But you know what Bill is.

Well, the husbands left on Saturday morning, and by eleven o'clock Ida, Alice and I were all at Carrie's. The change in her was simply startling. She looked like a willow wand. She'd put her hair low on her neck, and except for a touch of black on her eyelashes, and of course her lips coloured, she hadn't a speck of makeup on. She'd taken the pearls out of her ears, too, and she wore tennis clothes and flat-heeled shoes that made her look like a child.

She was sending the children off in the car as we went up the drive.

"They're off to mother's," she said. "I'll miss them frightfully, but this is a real lark, girls, and I can't imagine anything more killing to romance than small children."

She kissed the top of the baby's head, and he yelled like a trooper. Then the motor drove off, and, as Alice Warrington said, the stage was set.

"Get your tennis things on," Carrie said. "The men will be here for lunch."

We said with one voice that we wouldn't play tennis. Ie was too hot. She eyed us coldly.

"For heaven's sake," she said, "play up. Nobody asked you to play tennis. But if you are asked don't say it's too hot. Do any of the flappers at the club ever find it too hot to play? Sprain an ankle or break a racket, but don't talk about its being too violent, or that you've given it up the last few years. Try to remember that for two days you're in the game again, and don't take on a handicap to begin with."

Well, things started off all right, I'll have to admit that, although Carrie looked a trifle queer when Harry Delaney, getting out of the motor that had brought them from the station, held out a baby's rattle to her.

"Found it in the car," he said. "How are the youngsters anyhow?"

"Adorable!" said Carrie, and flung the rattle into the house.

Roger came straight to me and took both my hands.

"Upon my word, Clara," he said, "this is more luck than I ever expected again. Do you remember the last time we were all here together?"

"Of course I do." He was still holding my hands and I felt rather silly. But the others had paired off instantly and no one was paying any attention.

"I was almost suicidal that last evening. You—you had just told me, you know."

I withdrew my hands. When a man is being sentimental I like him to be accurately sentimental. It had been a full month after that house party, at a dance Carrie gave, that I had told him of my engagement to Bill. However, I said nothing and took a good look at Roger. He was wonderful.

Why is it that married men lose their boyishness, and look smug and sleek and domesticated almost before the honeymoon is over? Roger stood there with his hat in his hand and the hot noon sun shining on him. And he hadn't changed a particle, except that his hair was grey over his ears and maybe a bit thinner. He was just as eager, just as boyish, just as lean as he'd ever been. And positively he was handsomer than ever.

Bill is plain. He is large and strong, of course, but he says himself his face must have been cut out with an axe. "Rugged and true," he used to call himself. But lately, in spite of golf, he had put on weight.

Well, to get on.

Luncheon was gay. Everyone sat beside the person he wanted to sit beside, and said idiotic things, and Peter Arundel insisited on feeding Alice's strawberries to her one by one. Nobody talked bills or the high cost of living. Roger is a capital *raconteur*, and we laughed until we wept over his stories. I told some of Bill's stock jokes and they went with a hurrah. At three o'clock we were still at the table, and when Carrie asked the men if they wanted to run over to the Country Club for a couple of hours of golf Wilbur Bayne put the question to a vote and they voted "No" with a roar.

I remember that Harry Delaney said a most satisfactory thing just as luncheon was over.

"It's what I call a real party," he said. "After a man is thirty or thereabouts he finds débutantes still thrilling, of course, but not restful. They're always wanting to go somewhere or do something. They're too blooming healthy. The last week-end

I spent I danced until 4 A. M. and was wakened at seven-thirty by a fair young flower throwing gravel through my open window and inviting me to a walk before breakfast!"

"Anyone seen about the place before eleven to-morrow morning," said Carrie, "will be placed under restraint. For one thing, it would make the servants talk. They're not used to it."

So far so good. I'll confess freely that if they'd let me alone I'd never have thought of getting even. But you know Carrie Smith. She has no reserves. And she had to tell about my party and the way the husbands behaved.

"Don't glare, Clara," she said. "Your house is nice and your food and drink all that could be desired. But it was not a hilarious party, and I'll put it up to the others."

Then and there she told about the swimming and the golf and the knitting. The men roared. She exaggerated, of course. Bill did not go to sleep at dinner. But she made a good story of it, and I caught Roger's eye fixed on me with a look that said plainly that he'd always known I'd made a mistake, and here was the proof.

We went out into the garden and sat under a tree. But soon the others paired off and wandered about. Roger and I were left alone, and I was boiling.

"Don't look like that, little girl," said Roger, bending toward me. "It hurts me terribly to—to think you are not happy."

He put a hand over mine, and at that moment Alice Warrington turned from a rosebush she and Peter were pretending to examine, and saw me. She raised her eyebrows, and that gave me the idea. I put my free hand over Roger's and tried to put my soul into my eyes.

"Don't move," I said. "Hold the position for a moment, Roger, and look desperately unhappy."

"I am," he said. "Seeing you again brings it all back. Are they looking? Shall I kiss your hand?"

I looked over. Alice and Peter were still staring.

"Bend over," I said quickly, "and put your cheek against it. It's more significant and rather hopeless. I'll explain later."

He did extremely well. He bent over passionately until his head was almost in my lap, and I could see how carefully his hair was brushed over a thin place at the crown. Thank goodness, Bill keeps his hair anyhow!

"How's this?" he said in a muffled voice.

"That's plenty." I'd made up my mind, and I meant to go through with it. But I felt like a fool. There's something about broad daylight that makes even real sentiment look idiotic.

He sat up and looked into my eyes.

"There are times," he said, raising his voice, "when I feel I can't stand it. I'm desperately— desperately unhappy, Clara."

"We must make the best of things," I said, and let my eyes wander toward Alice and Peter. They had turned and were retreating swiftly through the garden.

"Now," said Roger, sitting back and smoothing his hair, "what's it all about?"

So I told him and explained my plan. Even now, when I never want to see him again, I must admit that Roger is a sport. He never turned a hair.

"Of course I'll do it. It isn't as hard as you imagine. Our meeting like this revives the old fire. I'm mad about you, recklessly mad, and you're crazy about me. All right so far. But a thing like that won't throw much of a crimp into Carrie. Probably she expects it."

"To-night," I explained, "we'll be together, but silent and moody. When we smile at their nonsense it is to be a forced smile. We're intent on ourselves. Do you see? And you might go to Carrie after dinner and tell her you think you'll go. You can't stand being near me. It's too painful. I'll talk to one of the men too."

He looked rather uncomfortable.

"Oh, I wouldn't do that, Clara. They wouldn't understand."

"Not about you," I retorted coldly. "I'll merely indicate that Bill and I aren't hitting it off, and that a woman has a right to be happy. Then, when things happen, they'll remember what I said."

He turned round his wicker chair so that he faced me.

"When things happen?" he said. "What things?"

"When we elope to-morrow night," I replied.

I'm not defending myself. Goodness knows I've gone through all that. I am merely explaining. And I think Roger deserves part of the blame, but of course the woman always suffers. If he had only been frank with me at the time it need never have happened. Besides, I've been back to that bridge again and again, and with ordinary intelligence and a hammer he could have repaired it. It is well enough for him to say he didn't have a hammer. He should have had a hammer.

At the mention of an elopement Roger changed colour, but I did not remember that until afterward. He came up to scratch rather handsomely, when he was able to speak, but he insisted that I write the whole thing to Bill.

"I can tell him afterward," I protested.

"That won't help me if he has beaten me up first. You write him to the office, so he'll get it Monday morning when he gets back from the game. If anything should slip up you're protected, don't you see?

Tell him it's a joke and why we're doing it. I—I hope Bill has kept his sense of humor."

Well, it looked simple enough. We were to act perfectly silly and moonstruck all the rest of that day and Sunday until we had them all thoroughly worried. Then on Sunday night we were to steal Wallie's car and run away in it. The through train stops at a station about four miles away, at eleven-fourteen at night, and we were to start that way and then turn around and go to mother's.

We planned it thoroughly, I must say. Roger said he'd get one of the fellows to cash a check for all the money he had about him. They'd be sure to think of that when Carrie got my note. And I made a draft of the note then and there on the back of an old envelope from Roger's pocket. We made it as vague as possible.

"Dear Carrie," it ran, "by the time you receive this I shall be on my way to happiness. Try to forgive me. I couldn't stand things another moment. We only live one life and we all make mistakes. Read Ellen Key and don't try to follow me. I'm old enough to know my own mind, and all you have been saying this last few days has convinced me that when a chance for happiness comes one is a fool not to take it. Had it not been for you I should never have had my eyes opened to what I've been missing all this time. I have wasted my best years, but at last I am being true to myself.   CLARA."

"Now," I said, rather viciously I dare say, "let her read that and throw a fit. She'll never again be able to accuse me of making things dull for her."

Roger read it over.

"We'd better write Bill's letter," he said, "and get it off. We—it wouldn't do to have Bill worried, you know."

So we went into the house and wrote Bill's letter. We explained everything—how stupid they'd all found our party and that this was only a form of revenge.

"Suppose," Roger said as I sealed it, "suppose they get excited and send for the police?"

That stumped us. It was one thing to give them a bad night, and telephone them in the morning that it was a joke and that I'd gone direct from Carrie's to mother's, which was the arrangement. But Carrie was a great one for getting in detectives. You remember, the time her sister was married, that Carrie had a detective in the house for a week before the wedding watching the presents, and how at the last minute the sister wanted to marry the detective, who was a good-looking boy, and they had a dreadful time getting her to the church.

We both thought intently for quite a time.

"We must cut the telephone wire, Roger," I said at length.

Roger was not eager about cutting the telephone. He said he would probably be shocked to death, although if he could find a pair of rubber overshoes he'd take the risk.

"It ought to be done the very last thing," he said. "No use rousing their suspicions early."

We played up hard all afternoon. Roger kissed the lump of sugar he put in my tea, and went and sulked on the parapet when Peter Arundel came and sat beside me. Carrie joined him there, and I could see her talking earnestly to him while Roger looked out over the landscape with eyes that were positively sombre.

"Having a good time?" said Peter Arundel to me.

"Heavenly, Peter," I replied, looking at Roger. "I didn't believe I could be so happy."

"Go to it," said Peter. "What's a day or two out of a lifetime."

I turned round and faced him, my hands gripped hard in my lap.

"That's it," I said tensely. "That's the thought that's killing me. One can only be happy for a day or two."

"Oh, I wouldn't go so far as that," said Peter. "You have a pretty fair time, you know, Clara. Old Bill's a good sort."

"Oh, Bill!" I said.

"I went to college with Bill. Maybe Bill hasn't any frills, but he's a real man." He glared at Roger's drooping shoulders. "He's no tailor's dummy anyhow."

I ignored this.

"Peter," I said in a thin voice, "have you ever read Ellen Key?"

"Not on your life!" said Peter.

I quoted a bit I happened to remember.

" 'Nothing is wiser than the modern woman's desire to see life with her own eyes, not only with those of a husband.' " I sighed.

"If I were Bill," said Peter, "I'd burn that book."

" 'Nothing,' " I continued, " 'is more true than that souls which are parted by a lack of perfect frankness never belonged to one another.' "

"Look here," said Peter, and got up; "I think you've lost your mind, Clara—you and Roger Waite both. Look at him mooning over there. I'd like to turn the garden hose on him."

I looked at Roger—a long gaze that made Peter writhe.

" 'Love's double heartbeat'——" I began. But Peter stalked away, muttering.

Carrie had left Roger, so I put down my cup and followed him to the parapet of the terrace.

"Darling!" he said. And then, finding Peter was not with me: "How's it going?"

"Cracking! They're all worried already."

"We've hardly started. Slip your arm through mine, Clara, and I'll hold your hand. Dear little hand!" he said. "When I think that instead of that ring——" Here he choked and kissed my hand. Then I saw that Harry Delaney was just below the wall.

Carrie's voice broke in on our philandering.

"If," she said coldly, "you two people can be pried apart with a crowbar for a sufficient length of time, we will motor to Bubbling Spring. There's just time before dinner."

"I don't think I'll go, Carrie," I said languidly. "I have a headache and Roger has just offered to read to me. Do you remember how you used to cure my headaches, Roger?"

"I'd rather not talk about those days, Clara," said Roger in a shaky voice.

"I wish you two people could see and hear yourselves!" Carrie cried furiously, and turned on her heel.

"I guess that will hold her for a while," Roger purred. "Clara, you're an angel and an inspiration. I haven't had such a good time since I had scarlet fever."

Dinner, which should have been gay, was simply

noisy. They were all worried, and it is indicative of how Carrie had forgotten her pose and herself that she wore her diamond necklace. Roger had been placed at the other end of the table from me, but he slipped in and changed the cards. There were half a dozen dinner guests, but Roger and I ate little or nothing.

"Act as though the thought of food sickens you," I commanded.

"But I'm starving!"

"I'll have my maid take a tray into the garden later."

In spite of me he broke over at the entrée, which was extremely good. But everyone saw that we were not eating. The woman on Roger's right, a visitor, took advantage of a lull in the noise to accuse Roger of being in love. Ida giggled, but Roger turned to his neighbour.

"I am in love," he said mournfully; "hopelessly, idiotically, madly, recklessly in love."

"With any particular person?"

"With you," said Roger, who had never seen her before.

She quite fluttered.

"But I am married!"

"Unfortunate, but not fatal," said Roger distinctly, while everyone listened. "These days one must be true to one's self."

We were awfully pleased with ourselves that evening. I said my head still ached and I could not dance. Roger and I sat out-of-doors most of the time, and at eleven o'clock Powell, my maid, brought out a tray of what was left from dinner and the dance supper. She took it by order to a small shaded porch off the billiard room, and we found her there with it.

"Thank you, Powell," I said. But Roger followed her into the house. When he returned he was grinning.

"Might as well do it right while we're about it," he observed. "To-morrow morning Powell will go to Carrie and tell her you sat up all night by the window, and she's afraid you are going to be ill."

In the dusk we shook hands over the tray.

Well, a lot of things happened, such as our overhearing the men in the billiard room debating about getting poor old Bill on the long distance.

"It isn't a flirtation," said Wilbur Bayne. "I've seen Clara flirting many a time. But this is different. They're reckless, positively reckless. When a man as fond of his stomach as Roger lets a whole meal go by, he's pretty far gone."

Roger bent over, with a part of a squab in his hand.

"Have they bitten!" he said. "They've not only

swallowed hook, line and sinker but they're walking up the bank to put themselves in the basket!"

Well, the next morning it was clear that the girls had decided on a course and were following it. Although it had been arranged that everyone was to sleep late, breakfast trays appeared in the rooms at nine-thirty, with notes asking us to go to church. When I said I had not slept, and did not care to go, no one went, and when Roger appeared at eleven the girls surrounded me like a cordon of police.

Roger was doing splendidly. He came up across the tennis court, covered with dust, and said he had not slept and had been walking since six o'clock. The men eyed him with positive ferocity.

I'll not go into the details of that day, except to relate a conversation Ida Elliott and I had after luncheon. She came into my room and closed the door behind her softly, as if I were ill.

"Well," she said, "I did think, Clara, that if you didn't have any sense, you would have some consideration for Carrie."

I had been addressing the envelope to Bill, and so I shoved a sheet of paper over it.

"I'm not going to try to read what you are writing," she said rudely.

"What do you mean about Carrie?"

"She's almost ill, that's all. How could anyone

have had any idea that Roger and you———" She fairly choked.

"Roger and I are only glad to be together again," I said defiantly. Then I changed to a wistful tone. Just hearing it made me sorry for myself. "We are old friends; Carrie knew that. It is cruel of you all to—to spoil the little bit of happiness I can get out of life."

"What about Bill?"

"Bill?" I said vaguely. "Oh—Bill! Well, Bill would never stand in the way of my being true to myself. He would want me to be happy."

I put my handkerchief suddenly to my eyes, and she gave me a scathing glance.

"I'm going to telephone Bill," she said. "You're not sane, Clara. And when you come back to your senses it may be too late."

She flounced out, and I knew she would call Bill if she could. From the window I could see that Harry Delaney had Roger by the arm and was walking him up and down. It was necessary, if the fun was to go on, to disconnect the telephone. I ran down to the library and dropped the instrument on the floor twice, but when I put it to my ear to see if it was still working I found it was, for Central was saying: "For the love of heaven, something nearly busted my eardrum!"

Ida had not come down yet, and the telephone

was on a table in the corner, beside a vase of flowers. When I saw the flowers I knew I was saved. I turned the vase over and let the water soak into the green cord that covers the wires. I knew it would short-circuit the telephone, for once one of the maids at home, washing the floor, had wet the cord, and we were cut off for an entire day.

During the afternoon I gave Harry Delaney the letter to Bill. Harry was going to the little town that was the post office to get something for Carrie.

"You won't forget to mail it, will you, Harry?" I asked in a pathetic voice.

He read the address and looked at me.

"What are you writing to Bill for, Clara? He'll be home in the morning."

I looked confused. Then I became frank.

"I'm writing him something I don't particularly care to tell him."

He fairly groaned and thrust the thing into his pocket.

"For refined cruelty and absolute selfishness," he said, "commend me to the woman with nothing to do but to get into mischief."

"Will you promise to mail it?"

"Oh, I'll mail it all right," he said; "but I give you until six o'clock this evening to think it over. I'm not going to the station until then."

"To think over what?" I asked, my eyes opened innocently wide. But he flung away in a fury.

It was rather fun that afternoon. If my party had been dreary on Sunday it was nothing to Carrie's. They'd clearly all agreed to stay round and keep Roger and me apart. Everybody sulked, and the men got the Sunday newspapers and buried themselves in them. Once I caught Roger dropping into a doze. He had refused the paper and had been playing up well, sitting back in his chair with his cap over his eyes and gazing at me until everybody wiggled.

"Roger," I called, when I saw his eyes closing, "are you game for a long walk?"

Roger tried to look eager.

"Sure," he said.

"Haven't you a particle of humanity?" Carrie demanded. She knew some of them would have to go along, and nobody wanted to walk. It was boiling. "He has been up since dawn and he's walked miles."

Roger ignored her.

"To the ends of the world—with you, Clara," he said, and got up.

In the end they all went. It was a tragic-looking party. We walked for miles and miles, and Carrie was carrying her right shoe when we got back. It was too late to dress for dinner, and everyone was worn out. So we went in as we were.

"I'm terribly sorry it's nearly over," I babbled as the soup was coming in. "It has been the most wonderful success, hasn't it? Ida, won't you have us all next week? Maybe we can send the husbands to the yacht races."

"Sorry," said Ida coldly; "I've something else on."

Worried as they were, nobody expected us to run away. How to let them know what had happened, and put a climax to their discomfiture, was the question. I solved it at last by telling Powell to come in at midnight with the sleeping medicine Carrie had given her for me. I knew, when she found I was not there, she would wait and at last raise the alarm. What I did not know was that she would come in half an hour early, and cut off our lead by thirty minutes.

The evening dragged like the afternoon, and so thoroughly was the spice out of everything for them all, that when I went upstairs at ten-thirty Ida Elliott was singing Jim's praises to Wilbur Bayne, and Carrie had got out the children's photographs and was passing them round.

As I went out through the door Roger opened for me, he bowed over my hand and kissed it.

"Oh, cut it out!" I heard Peter growl, and there was a chorus from the others.

I had to stop in the hall outside and laugh. It was the last time I laughed for a good many hours.

By eleven I was ready. Everyone was upstairs, and Carrie had found out about the telephone by trying to call up her mother to inquire about the children. I had packed a small suitcase and at Roger's whistle I was to drop it out the window to him. Things began to go wrong with that, for just as I was ready to drop it someone rapped at my door. I swung it too far out, and it caught Roger full in the chest and carried him over backward. I had just time to see him disappear in the shrubbery with a sort of dull thud when Alice Warrington knocked again.

She came in and sat on the bed.

"I don't want to be nasty, Clara," she said, "but you know how fond I am of you, and I don't want you to misunderstand Roger. It's his way to make violent love to people and then get out. Of course you know he's being very attentive to Maisie Brown. She's jealous of you now. Somebody told her Roger used to be crazy about you. If she hears of this——"

"Clara!" said Roger's voice under the window.

Alice rose, with the most outraged face I've ever seen.

"He is positively shameless," she said. "As for you, Clara, I can't tell you how I feel."

"Clara!" said Roger. "I must speak to you. Just one word."

Alice swept out of the room and banged the door. I went to the window.

"Something seems to have broken in the dratted thing," he said. "It smells like eau de Cologne. I'm covered with it."

As it developed later it was eau de Cologne. I have never got a whiff of it since that I don't turn fairly sick. And all of that awful night Roger fairly reeked with it.

Well, by midnight everything was quiet, and I got downstairs and into the drive without alarming anyone. Roger was waiting, and for some reason or other—possibly the knock—he seemed less enthusiastic.

"I hope Harry remembered the letter to Bill," he said. "Whether this thing is a joke or not depends on the other person's sense of humor. What in heaven's name made you put scent in your bag?"

He had his car waiting at the foot of the drive, and just as I got in we heard it thunder.

"How far is it to your mother's?"

"Twelve miles."

"It's going to rain."

"Rain or not, I'm not going back, Roger," I said. "Imagine Bill's getting that letter for nothing."

He got into the car and it began to rain at once. Everyone knows about that storm now. We had gone about four miles when the sky fairly opened. The water beat in under the top and washed about our feet. We drove up to the hubs in water, and the lights, instead of showing us the way, only lit up a wall of water ahead. It was like riding into Niagara Falls. We were pretty sick, I can tell you.

"Why didn't you look at the sky?" I yelled at Roger, above the beating of the storm. "Bill can always tell when it's going to storm."

"Oh, damn Bill!" said Roger, and the car slid off the road and into a gully. Roger just sat still and clutched the wheel.

"Aren't you going to do something?" I snapped. "I'm not going to sit here all night and be drowned."

"Is there anything you could suggest?"

"Can't you get out and push it?"

"I cannot."

But after five minutes or so he did crawl out, and by tying my suitcase straps round one of the wheels he got the car back into the road. I daresay I was a trifle pettish by that time.

"I wish you wouldn't drip on me," I said.

"I beg your pardon," he replied, and moved as far from me as he could.

We went on in silence. At last:

"There's one comfort about getting that soaking," he said: "it's washed that damned perfume off."

There's one thing about Bill, he keeps his temper. And he doesn't raise the roof when he gets his clothes wet. He rather likes getting into difficulties, to show how well he can get out of them. But Roger is like a cat. He always hated to get his feet wet.

"If you had kept the car in the centre of the road you wouldn't have had to get out," I said shortly.

"Oh, well, if you're going back to first causes," he retorted, "if you'd never suggested this idiotic thing I wouldn't be laying up a case of lumbago at this minute."

"Lumbago is middle-aged, isn't it?"

"We're neither of us as young as we were a few years ago."

That was inexcusable. Roger is at least six years older than I am. Besides, even if it were true, there was no necessity for him to say it. But there was no time to quarrel, for at that moment we were going across a bridge over a small stream. It was a river now. The first thing I knew was that the car shook and rocked and there was a dull groaning underneath. The next minute we had gone slowly down about four feet and the creek was flowing over us.

We said nothing at first. The lights went off al-

most immediately, as the engine drowned, and there
we sat in the flood, and the first thing I knew I
was crying.

"The bridge is broken," said Roger, above the
rush of the stream.

"I didn't think you were washing the car," I
whimpered. "We'll be drowned, that's all."

The worst of the storm was over, but as far as I
was concerned it might just as well have been pouring. When Roger got his matches and tried to light
one it only made a sick streak of phosphorescence on
the side of the box. To make things worse, Roger
turned round, and where the road crossed the brow
of the hill behind us there was the glow of automobile lamps. He swore under his breath.

"They're coming, Clara," he said. "That fool of
a maid didn't wait until midnight."

The thought of being found like that, waist-deep
in water, drove me to frenzy. I knew how they'd
laugh, how they'd keep on laughing for years.
They'd call us the Water Babies probably, or something equally hateful. I just couldn't stand the
thought.

I got up.

"Let them think we're drowned—anything," I
said desperately. "I will not be found like this."

Roger looked about like a hunted animal.

"There's—there's a house near here on the hill,"

he said. Afterward I remembered how he hesitated
over it. "We could get up there, I'm pretty sure."

He looked back.

"They seem to have stopped," he said. "Perhaps
the other bridge has gone."

He lifted me out and set me on the bank. He
was not particularly gentle about it, and I was all
he could carry. That's one thing about Bill—he's
as strong as an ox and as gentle as a young gazelle.

Well, we scurried up the bank, the water pouring
off us, and I lost a shoe. Roger wouldn't wait until
I found it, but dragged me along, panting. Suddenly I knew that I hated him with a deadly hatred.
The thought of how nearly I had married him made
me shiver.

"I wish you'd let go of me," I said.

"Why? You can't climb alone in the silly clothes
you wear."

"Perhaps not, but I don't like you to touch me."

"Oh, if you feel like that——" He let me go,
and I almost fell. "You know, Clara, I am trying
hard to restrain myself, but—this is all your doing."

"I suppose I broke the bridge down," I said bitterly, "and brought on the rain, and all the rest
of it."

"Now I recognise the Clara I used to know," he
had the audacity to say, "always begging the question and shifting the responsibility. For heaven's

sake don't stop to quarrel! They've probably found the car by this time."

We got to the house and I fell exhausted on the steps. To my surprise Roger got out a bunch of keys and fitted one to the lock.

"I know these people," he said. "I—I sometimes come out in the fall for a bit of shooting. Place is closed now."

The interior looked dark and smelled musty. I didn't want to go in, but it was raining again and there was nothing else to do.

"Better overcome your repugnance and give me your hand," he said. "If we turn on a light they'll spot us."

Oh, it is all very well to say, looking back, that we should have sat in the car until we were found, and have carried it all off as a part of the joke. I couldn't, that's flat. I couldn't have laughed if I'd been paid to.

We bumped into a square hall and I sat down. It was very quiet all at once, and the only thing to be heard was the water dripping from us to the hardwood floor.

"If that's a velvet chair you're on it will be ruined," said Roger's voice out of the darkness.

"I hope it is. Where is the telephone?"

"There is a telephone closet under the stairs."

"You know a lot about this house. Whose is it?"

"It's the Brown place. You know it."

"Maisie Brown's!"

"Yes." He was quite sullen.

"And you have a key like one of the family! Roger, you are engaged to her!"

"I was," he said. "The chances are when this gets out I won't be."

I don't know why now, but it struck me as funny. I sat and laughed like a goose, and the more I laughed the harder Roger breathed.

"You've got to see me through this, Clara," he said at last. "You can't telephone Carrie—you've fixed all that. But you can get your mother. Tell her the circumstances and have her send a car for you. I'll stay here to-night. And if you take my advice you'll meet Bill at the train to-morrow morning and beat Carrie to it. She'll be in town with a line of conversation by daybreak."

He found some dry matches and led me to the telephone. Something in the way I dripped, or because I padded across the floor in one stocking foot, made him a trifle more human.

"I'll close the curtains and light the log fire," he said. "Things are bad enough without your taking pneumonia."

The moment I took the receiver off the hook I knew the wires were down somewhere. I sat for a moment, then I opened the door. Roger was on his knees lighting the fire. He looked very thin, with his clothes stuck to him, and the hair that he wore brushed over the bare place had been washed down, and he looked almost bald.

"Roger," I said, with the calmness of despair, "the wires are down!"

"Hush," said Roger suddenly. "And close that door."

It seemed rather foolish to me at the time. Since they had followed us, they'd know perfectly well that if Roger was there I was.

In walked Maisie Brown and about a dozen other people!

I can still hear the noise they made coming in, and then a silence, broken by Maisie's voice.

"Why, Roger!" she said.

"Awfully surprising to see you here—I mean, I expect you are surprised to see me here," said Roger's voice, rather thin and stringy. "The fact is, I was going by, and—it was raining hard, and I——"

"Then that was your car in the creek?"

"Well, yes," Roger admitted, after a hesitation. He was evidently weighing every word, afraid of committing himself to anything dangerous.

"I thought you were at Carrie Smith's."

"I was on my way home."

Everybody laughed. It was about a dozen miles to Roger's road home from Carrie's.

"Come on, now, there's a mystery. Own up," said a man's voice. "Where's the beautiful lady? Drowned?"

Luckily no one waited for an answer. They demanded how he had got in, and when he said he had a key they laughed again. Some one told Maisie she might as well confess. If Roger had a key to the house it required explanation.

If ever I heard cold suspicion in a girl's voice, it was in Maisie's when she answered:

"Oh, we're engaged all right, if that's what you mean," she said. "But I think Roger and I——"

They didn't give her a chance to finish, the idiots! They gave three cheers, and then, as nearly as I could make out, they formed a ring and danced round them. They'd been to a picnic somewhere, and as the bridges were down they were there for the night.

Do you think they went to bed?

Not a bit of it. They found some canned things in a pantry, and fixed some hot drinks and drank to Maisie and Roger. And I sat in the telephone closet and tried not to sneeze.

I sat there for two hours.

About two o'clock I heard Maisie say she would have to telephone home, and if a totally innocent

person can suffer the way I did I don't know how
a guilty one could live. But Roger leaped in front
of her.

"I'll do it, honey," he said. "I—I was just thinking of telephoning."

They were close to the door.

"Don't call me honey," Maisie said in a tense
voice. "I know about Carrie Smith's party and who
was there. After the way Clara has schemed all these
years to get you back, to have you fall into a trap
like that! It's sickening!"

She put her hand on the knob of the door.

"Listen, darling," Roger implored. "I—I don't
care a hang for anyone but you. I'm perfectly
wretched. I——"

He pulled her hand off the knob of the door and
I heard him kiss it.

"Let me call your mother," he said. "She'll know
you are all right when I'm here."

Well, I had to listen. The idea of her saying I'd
tried to get him back, when everybody knows how
he carried on when I turned him down! I hadn't
given him a thought for years.

"Did you make love to Clara?"

"Certainly not. Look here, Maisie, you can afford to be magnanimous. Clara's a nice woman, but
she's years older than you are. You know who loves
you, don't you?"

Positively he was appealing. He sounded fairly sick.

"Get mother on the wire," said Maisie curtly. "Then call me. I'll talk to her."

Roger opened the door as soon as she had gone and squeezed in beside me.

"She's coming to telephone. You'll have to go somewhere else, Clara," he said.

"Where, for instance?"

"I may be able to collect them in the pantry. Then you can run across and get out the door."

"Into the rain?"

"Well, you can't stay here, can you?"

"I'll do nothing of the sort. Go and tell her the wires are down. They are. And then get that crowd of flappers upstairs. If they go the men will. I give you ten minutes. At the end of that time I'm coming out to the fire. I'm cold."

"And after they go up, what?"

"Then you're going into somebody's room to steal me a pair of dry shoes. Get Maisie's, she's about my size. We'll have to walk to mother's."

"I can't leave, Clara. If anything happened and I was missing——"

When I said nothing he knew I was in earnest. He went out and told them the telephone was out of order, and somehow or other he shooed them upstairs. I opened the door of the telephone closet for air, and I could hear them overhead, ragging Roger about the engagement and how he happened to get to Maisie's when it was so far from his road home. Every time I thought they were settled, some fool of a boy or giggling débutante would come down again and look for soap, or towels, or matches, or heaven knows what. I could have strangled the lot of them.

By three o'clock it was fairly quiet, and I crept out and sat by the log fire. If I had had a shoe I would have started off then and there. I'm no coward and I was desperate. But I couldn't go in my silk stockings. And when after a while Roger slipped down the stairs he had no shoes for me.

"I've tried all the girls' doors," he said wretchedly, "and they're locked. Couldn't you tie a towel round your foot, or something? I'm going to get into trouble over this thing yet. I feel it."

"Go up and bring me little Teddy Robinson's shoes," I snapped. "It won't compromise you to go into his room, I daresay."

"What if he's not asleep?"

"Tell him you're going to clean them. Tell him anything. And, Roger, don't let Maisie pull the *ingénue* stunt on you. I may be years older than she is, but Maisie's no child."

Well, with everyone gone and Roger hunting me some boots, I felt rather better. I went to the pantry

and fixed some hot milk and carried it in to drink
by the fire. Roger came down with the boots, and
to save time he laced them on my feet while I sat
back and sipped.

That, of course, in spite of what Bill pretends to
think, is why Roger was on his knees before me
when Peter walked in.

Oh, yes, Peter Arundel walked in! It just shows
the sort of luck I played in that night. He walked
in and slammed the door.

"Thank heaven!" he said, and stalked over to
me and jerked the cup out of my hand. "You
pair of idiots!" he fairly snarled. "What sort of
an escapade is this anyhow?"

"It—it's a joke, Peter," I quavered. He stared
at me in speechless scorn. "Positively it is a joke,
Peter."

"I daresay," he said grimly. "Perhaps to-morrow I may see it that way. The question is, will
Bill think it's a joke?"

He looked round, and luckily for me he saw all
the girls' wraps lying about.

"If the family's here, Clara," he said in a milder
voice, "I—I may be doing you an injustice."

Roger had not said a word. He was standing in
front of the fire, watching the stairs.

"When we found the note," Peter went on in his
awful booming voice, "saying you were going at last

to be true to yourself, and when you and Roger had disappeared, what were we to think? Especially after the way you two had fallen into each other's arms from the moment you met."

"How interesting!" said a voice from the staircase.

It was Maisie!

Well, what's the use of going into it again? She gave Roger his ring instantly, and Roger was positively grey. He went back on me without a particle of shame—said I'd suggested the whole thing and begged him to help me; that he'd felt like a fool the whole time.

"Maisie, darling," he said, "surely you know that there's nobody in all the world for me but you."

He held out the ring to her, but she shook her head.

"I'm not angry—not any more," she said. "I've lost my faith in you, that's all. One thing I'm profoundly grateful for—that you and Clara had this —this explosion before we were married and not after."

"Maisie!" he cried.

All at once I remembered Bill's letter, which would positively clear us. But Peter said Harry Delaney's coat had been stolen from the machine, letter and all! Maisie laughed at that, as if she didn't believe there had been such a letter, and

Roger went a shade greyer. All at once it came to me that now Bill would never forgive me. He is so upright, Bill is, and he expects everyone to come up to his standard. And in a way Bill had always had me on a pedestal, and he would never believe that I had been such a fool as to jump off for a lark.

Maisie turned and walked upstairs, leaving the three of us there, Roger holding the ring and staring at it with a perfectly vacant face. At last he turned and went to the door.

"Where are you going, Roger?" I asked helplessly.

"I'm going out to drown myself," he said, and went out.

I shall pass over the rest briefly. Peter took me home in his car. I did not go to mother's. For one thing, the bridge was down. For another, it seemed better for Bill and me to settle things ourselves without family interference.

I went home and went to bed, and all day Monday I watched for Bill. Powell came over and I put on my best negligée and waited, with a water bottle to keep my feet warm and my courage up.

He did not come.

I stayed in bed for three days, and there was not a sign from him. Carrie and Ida telephoned, but only formal messages, and Alice Warrington sent me a box of flowers with her card. But Bill did not come home or call up. I knew he must be staying at the club, and I had terrible hours when I knew he would never forgive me, and then there would be a divorce, and I wanted to die. Roger never gave a sign, but he had not drowned himself.

Wednesday evening came, and no Bill. By that time I knew it was Bill or nobody for me. After those terrible two days at Carrie's, the thought of Bill's ugly, quiet face made me perfectly homesick for him. I didn't care how much he fell asleep in the evening after dinner. That only showed how contented he was. And I tried to imagine being married to Roger, and seeing him fuss about his ties, and brush the hair over the thin places on top of his head, and I simply couldn't.

It was Wednesday evening when I heard a car come up the drive. I knew at once that it was Bill. I had barely time to turn out all the lights but the pink-shaded one by the bed, and to lay a handkerchief across my eyes, when he came in.

"Well, Clara," he said, standing just inside the door, "I thought we'd better talk this over."

"Bill!" I said, from under the handkerchief.

"I should have come out sooner," he said without moving, "but at first I could not trust myself. I needed a little time."

"Who told you?"

"That doesn't matter, does it? Everybody knows

it. But that's not the question. The real issue is between you and me and that—that nincompoop, Waite."

"What has Roger got to do with it?" I looked out from under the handkerchief, and he was livid, positively.

"Bill," I said desperately, "will you come over and sit down on the side of the bed and let me tell you the whole story?"

"I won't be bamboozled, Clara; this is serious. If you've got anything to say, say it. I'll sit here."

He sat down just inside the door on a straight chair and folded his long arms. It was a perfectly hopeless distance.

"Bill!" I said appealingly, and he came over and sat, very uncompromising and stiff, on the side of the bed. I put out my hand, and after a moment's hesitation he took it, but I must say without enthusiasm. I felt like the guiltiest wretch unhung. That's what makes me so perfectly furious now.

"You see, Bill," I said, "it was like this." And I told him the whole thing. About halfway through he dropped my hand.

"It's been an awful lesson, Bill," I ended up. "I'll never say a word again about your enjoying yourself the way you want to. You can swim and play golf and shoot all you like, and—and sleep after dinner, if you'll only forgive me. Bill, suppose I had married Roger Waite!"

He drew a long breath.

"So that was it, old dear!" he said. "Well, all right. We'll put the whole thing in the discard." And he leaned over and put his arms round me.

That ought to be the end of the story. I'd had a lesson and so had some of the others. As Carrie Smith said afterward, to have a good time is one thing, but to be happy is entirely different, and the only way to be happy is to be smug and conventional and virtuous. I never say anything when she starts that line of conversation. But once or twice I've caught her eye, and she has had the grace to look uneasy.

But that's not all. There is more to the story, and now and then I eye Bill, and wonder when he will come and tell me the whole thing. For the other day, in the back of Bill's chiffonier, I came across the letter to him Harry Delaney said he had lost. And Bill had received it Monday morning!

That is not all. Clamped to it was a note from Peter Arundel, and that is why I am writing the whole story, using names and everything. It was a mean trick, and if Bill wants to go to Maisie Brown's wedding he can go. I shall not.

This is Peter's note:

"*Dear Old Man:* Inclosed is the letter Clara gave Delaney to mail, which I read to you last night over the long-distance phone. I'm called away or I'd bring it round.

"It was easy enough for you to say not to let Clara get away with it, but for a time during the storm it looked as if she'd got the bit and was off. Luckily their car got stuck in the creek, and the rest was easy. We saw them, during a flash of lightning, climbing the hill to the Brown place for shelter. Luck was with us after that, for Maisie and a crowd came along, and we told Maisie the story. I take my hat off to Maisie. She's a trump. If you could have seen Roger Waite's face when she gave him back the ring! Carrie, who was looking through the windows with the others, was so sorry for him that she wanted to go in and let him cry on her shoulder.

"I hope Clara didn't take cold. She must have been pretty wet. But you were quite right. It wasn't only that she'd have had the laugh on all of us if she got away with it. As you said, it would be a bad precedent.

"Burn this, for the love of Mike. If Clara sees it she'll go crazy.   Yours,   PETER."

THE BORROWED HOUSE

THE BORROWED HOUSE

I

"AND the things the balloon man said!" observed Daphne, stirring her tea. Daphne is my English cousin, and misnamed. "He went too high and Poppy's nose began to bleed."

"It poured," Poppy confirmed plaintively to me. "I leaned over the edge of the basket and it poured. And the next day the papers said it had rained blood in Tooting and that quantities of people had gone to the churches!" Poppy is short and wears her hair cut close and curled with an iron all over her head. She affects plaids.

"Then," Daphne went on, addressing the room in general, "he let some gas out of the bag and we began to settle. But just when we were directly over the Tower he grew excited and threw out sand. He said he wasn't going to hang his balloon on the Houses of Parliament like a penny ornament on a Christmas tree. And then the wind carried us north and we missed it altogether."

Mrs. Harcourt-Standish took a tea-cake. I was

sea-sick," she remarked pensively, "and he was unpleasant about that, too. It was really mountain sickness, although, of course, there wasn't any mountain. When we began to throw out the handbills he asked if I had swallowed *them*, too."

Mrs. Harcourt-Standish plays up the feminine. She is slim and blond, and wears slinky clothes and a bang—only they call it a fringe—across her forehead. She has been in prison five times and is supposed to have influence with the Cabinet. She showed me a lot of photographs of herself in the dock and in jail, put up in a frame that was made to represent a barred window. It was Violet Harcourt-Standish, you remember, who broke up the meeting of the Woman's Liberty League, the rival Suffragette association, by engaging the suite below their rooms, burning chemicals in the grates, and sending in a fire alarm when the smoke poured out of the windows.

I had been in England visiting Daphne for four months while Mother went to Italy, and I had had a very queer time. One was apt to go shopping with Daphne and end up on a carriage block or the box of a hansom cab, passing out handbills about votes for women. And once, when we dressed in our best gowns and went to a reception for the Cabinet, or something of the kind, Daphne stood on the stairs and began to make a speech. It turned out that she hadn't been invited at all and they put her out immediately—politely, but firmly. I slid away into the crowd, quite pale with the shock and disgrace, and stood in a corner, waiting to be arrested and searched for the spoons. But for a long time no one noticed me. Then a sunburned gentleman who was passing in the crowd saw me, hesitated and came back.

"I beg pardon," he said, and my heart turned entirely over, "but I think you came with Miss Wyndham? If you will allow me——"

"I am afraid you have made a mistake," I replied frigidly, with my lips stiff with fright. He bowed at that and passed on, but not before he had looked straight into my eyes and read the lie there.

After ages I left the window where I had taken shelter and got somehow to the dressing-room. Of course, Daphne had taken the carriage, so I told a sad-eyed maid that I was ill and would not wait for my brougham, and to call a cab. I was perfectly numb with rage when I got to Daphne's apartment, and burst in like a whirlwind. But Daphne was not at home. She came in at three that morning, maudlin with triumph, and found me asleep on the floor in my ball-gown, with a half-packed trunk before me.

She brought me tea and toast herself the next morning and offered it on her knees, which means something for Daphne—she is very stout and almost unbendable—and explained that I had been her patent of respectability, and that it had been a *coup;* that Mrs. Langley, of the Woman's Liberty League, had hired as a maid for the reception and had never got her foot out of the dressing-room! Red hair? Yes. And when I told Daphne that Mrs. Langley had helped me into my wrap she got up heavily and hopped three steps one way and three another, which is the way Daphne dances with joy.

I am afraid I have digressed. It is much harder to write a thing than to tell it. I used to write stories for our Journal at school and the girls were mad over them. But they were love stories, and this one deals with English politics and criminals— yes, you might call it a crime story. Of course there is love, too, but it comes in rather unexpectedly.

I left Daphne hopping three steps each way in triumph. Well, after that she did not take me around with her, although her friends came in and talked about The Cause to me quite often. And gradually I began to see that there was something to it, and why, if I paid taxes, shouldn't I vote? And hadn't I as much intelligence as the cab drivers and street sweepers? And why couldn't I will my money to my children if I ever had any?—children, not money. Of course, as Father pointed out after- ward, I should have been using my abilities in

America; but most of the American women I knew were so cravenly and abjectly contented. But even after my conversion Daphne would not take me in the balloon. She said I represented too much money to risk dumping in the Thames or hanging on a chimney.

The meeting at Daphne's was mainly to talk over the failure of the balloon ascension and to plan something new. But the actual conspiracy that followed was really an accident. It came about in the most casual way.

Violet Harcourt-Standish got up and went to the mirror to put on her veil, and some of the people began to gather their wraps.

"I'm tired," Daphne said suddenly. "We don't seem to get anywhere. We always come out the door we go in."

"Sometimes forcibly," Poppy said to me aside.

"And I haven't been strong, you know, since last summer," Daphne went on. Everybody nodded sympathetically. Daffie had raised a disturbance when Royalty was laying a cornerstone and had been jailed for it. (They put her to making bags and she sewed "Votes for Women" in white thread on every bag she made.) "I am going to take Madge down to Ivry for a week." I am Madge.

Violet turned from the mirror and raised her eyebrows. "Ivry!" she said. "How familiar it sounds!

Do you remember, Daphne, when pressure at the Hall became too strong for me, how I used to ride over to Ivry and have hysterics in the Tudor Room? And how once I wept on your Louis-Seize divan and had to have the purple stains bleached off my face? You lived a sort of vicarious matrimonial existence in those days, didn't you?"

Whatever she may have done to the Louis-Seize divan in earlier days, she was cheerful enough now, and I hailed her with delight.

"Do you live near Ivry?" I exclaimed. "How jolly!" That is English; I am frightfully English in my speech after a few weeks in London."

Somebody laughed and Daphne chuckled. It isn't especially feminine to chuckle, but neither is Daphne.

"My dear child," Mrs. Harcourt-Standish said, turning to me, "Harcourt Hall is closed. Mr. Harcourt is no longer my husband. The one is empty, the other in Canada"—vague, but rhetorical—"I have forgotten them both." There was nothing ambiguous about that. "I recall the house as miles from everything that was joyful. I shall always regard my being taken there as nothing short of kidnapping."

Then—she stopped short and glanced at Daphne. From Daphne her eyes travelled to Ernestine Sutcliffe, who put down her teacup with a clatter. There was a sudden hushed silence in the room; then Lady Jane Willoughby, who had been tying her motor veil, took it off and folded it in her lap. The Staffords, Poppy and her mother, exchanged glances. Without in the least understanding it I saw that something psychological was happening.

"Why not?" said Daphne quietly, looking around. "The house is still furnished, isn't it, Violet? And I suppose you could get in?"

Violet shrugged her shoulders. "I dare say; as I recall it, one could enter any one of the doors by merely leaning against it. The place is a million years old."

Everybody talked at once for a few minutes. I gave up trying to understand and took a fresh teacake. Then I noticed Lady Willoughby. In all that militant body, whatever adventure was afoot, hers was the only craven soul. She was picking at her veil with nervous fingers.

"I—don't you think it is very radical?" she ventured when she could be heard. Here Mrs. Stafford objected to the word "radical," and she substituted "revolutionary." "I should not wish anything to happen to him. He was a great friend of Willoughby's mother while she lived."

"That's all right among ourselves, Jane," Mrs. Stafford put in, "but if I recall the circumstances I wouldn't lay any emphasis on *that*. Anyhow, we don't intend to murder the man."

Lady Jane was only partially reassured. "Of course, you wouldn't mean to," she retorted, "but there is no use asking me to forget what Poppy Stafford did to the president of the Board of Trade last summer."

Poppy glanced up and shook her curls. "You are envious, Willieboy," she said, and put four lumps of sugar in her tea. "Willieboy" is Lady Willoughby's affectionate diminutive. They had started the tea all over again and I rather edged away from Poppy, but Daphne said afterward it was only a matter of a chair Poppy threw from the gallery at a public meeting, and that the man it fell on was only a secretary to the president of the Board of Trade.

Finally, I made out what the plan was, and mentally during the rest of the meeting I was making bags in jail.

They were going to abduct the Prime Minister!

Lady Jane had stopped looking back and had put her hand to the plow. (This sounds well, so I won't cut it out; but wasn't it Lot's wife that looked back? And wasn't that before the day of plows? Or *was* it?) And it was she who finally settled the whole thing, for it seems that the P. M. had confided to Lord Willoughby that the town was so noisy with Suffragettes that he could not find a quiet spot for a rubber of bridge; that since the balloon incident he slept in his clothes with the windows shut and locked; and that since the latest kitchen-maid had turned out to be the Honourable Maude Twombley, who slipped handbills into his entrées and served warnings in his dessert, he was going to travel, incognito and alone, to his daughter's place, The Oaks, outside of West Newbury, and get a little sleep.

And West Newbury was only four miles from the empty Harcourt Hall! In short, as Daphne succinctly put it: "Our Jonah was about to jump voluntarily overboard from the ship of state into the whaleboned jaws of the Suffragette whale."

Everybody went mad at that point, but as they grew excited I got cold. It began with my toes and went all over me.

Ernestine Sutcliffe stood on one of Daphne's tulip-wood and marquetry chairs and made a speech, gesticulating with her cup and dripping tea on me. And then somebody asked me to stand up and say what I thought. (I have never really spoken in public, but I always second the motions in a little club I belong to at home. It is a current-events club —so much easier to get the news that way than to read the newspaper.)

So I got up and made a short speech. I said: "I am only a feeble voice in this clamour of outraged womanhood against the oppressor, Man. I believe in the franchise for women, the ballot instead of the ballet. But at home, in America, when we want to take a bath we don't jump off the Brooklyn Bridge into the East River to do it."

Then I sat down. Daphne was raging.

"You are exceedingly vulgar," she said, "but since you insist on that figure of speech, you in America have waited a long time for the bath, and if you continue your present methods you won't get it before you need it."

II

Now that they had thought of it, they were all frantic for fear Mrs. Cobden-Fitzjames and the Woman's Liberty League might think of it, too, kidnap the Prime Minister, and leave us a miserable president of the Local Government Board or a wretched under-secretary of something or other.

The plan we evolved before the meeting broke up was to send a wire to Mrs. Gresham, the Premier's daughter, that he had been delayed, and to meet a later train. Then, Daphne's motor would meet the proper train—he was to arrive somewhere between seven and eight in the evening—carry his Impressiveness to Harcourt Hall and deliver him into the hands of the enemy. As Violet Harcourt-Standish voiced it: the motor gone, the railway miles away, what can he do? He will keep awake, because he will have slept in the train going down, and we can give him a cold supper. Nothing heavy to make him drowsy. Perhaps it would be better not to give him anything. (Hear! Hear!) Then, six speeches, each an hour long. At the end of that time we can promise him something to eat and a machine to take him to West Newbury on one condition. Every one looked up. "He must sign an indorsement of Suffrage for Women." (Loud applause.)

"Why not have a table laid," I suggested, "and show it to him? Let him smell it, so to speak. Visualise your temptation. You know,—'And the devil——' "

"This is the Prime Minister, Madge," Daphne broke in shortly, "and you are not happy in your Scriptural references."

Things went along with suspicious smoothness. Daphne really took the onus of the whole thing, and, of course, I helped her.

We all got new clothes, for everybody knows that if you can attract a man's eye you can get and maybe hold his ear. And Daphne wrote a fresh speech, one she had thought out in jail. It began, "Words! Words!! Words!!!" She wrote a poem, too, called the Song of the Vote, with the meter of the Song of a Shirt, and she wanted me to recite it, but even before I read it I refused.

The gown Mother had ordered for me at Paquin's on her way to the Riviera came just in time, a nice white thing over silver, with a square-cut neck and bits of sleeves made of gauze and silver fringe. Daphne got a pink velvet, although she is stout and inclined to be florid. She had jet butterflies embroidered over it, a flight of them climbing up one side of her skirt and crawling to the opposite shoulder, so that if one stood off at a distance she had a curiously diagonal appearance, as if she had listed heavily to one side.

By hurrying we got to Ivry on Thursday evening, and I was in a blue funk. Daphne was militantly cheerful, and, in the drawing-room after dinner, she put the finishing touches to her speech. It was warm and rainy, and I wandered aimlessly around, looking at hideous English photographs and wondering if picking oakum in an English jail was worse than making bags—and if they could arrest me, after all. Could they touch an American citizen? (But was I an American citizen? Perhaps I should have been naturalised, or something of that kind!) And I thought of Mother at Florence, in the villa on the Via Michelangelo—Mother, who classes Suffragists with Anti-Vaccinationists and Theosophists.

I would have gone up to bed, but that meant a candle and queer, shaky shadows on the wall; so I stayed with Daphne and looked at the picture of a young man in a uniform.

"Basil Harcourt," Daphne said absently, with a pen in her mouth, when I asked about it. "Taken years ago before he became an ass. How do you spell 'Supererogation'?"

"I haven't an idea," I admitted. "I don't even know what it means. I always confuse it with 'eleemosynary'." Daphne grunted. "Do you mean that this is Violet's husband?"

"It was—her first. Don't ask me about him: he always gives me indigestion. The man's mad! He stood right in this room, where he had eaten my ginger-cakes all his life and where he came to show me his first Eton collar and long trousers, and told me that he expected The Cause for his wife to be himself, and if she would rather raise hell for women than a family of children she would have to choose at once. And Violet stood just where you are, Madge, and retorted that maternity was not a Cause, and that any hen in the barnyard could raise a family.

"'I suppose you want to crow,' Basil said furiously, and slammed out. He went to Canada very soon after."

"Then perhaps he won't like our using his house for such a purpose. If he isn't in sympathy——"

"Twaddle," Daphne remarked, poising her pen

to go on. "In the first place, it isn't a house—it's a rattletrap; and in the second place, he won't know a thing about it."

It was all very tragic. I was thinking of them when I went out on the terrace in Daphne's mackintosh. The air was damp and sticky, but it was better than Daphne's conversation. I stood in the fountain court, leaning against a column and listening to the spray as it blew over on to the caladium leaves.

I am not sure just when I saw the figure. First it was part of the gloom, a deeper shadow in the misty garden. I saw it, so to speak, out of the tail of my eye. When I looked directly there was nothing there. Finally, I called softly over my shoulder to Daphne, but she did not hear. Instead, the shadow disengaged itself, moved forward and resolved into Bagsby, Daphne's chauffeur.

"I wasn't sure at first that you saw me, Miss," he said, touching his cap. "It's my turn until midnight; Clarkson 'as it until three, and the gardener until daylight."

"Good gracious!" I gasped. "Do you mean you are guarding the house?"

"Perhaps it's more what you would call surveillance," he said cautiously, "the picture gallery being over your head, Miss, and an easy job from the conservatory roof. We 'aven't told Miss Wyndham, yet, Miss, but the Wimberley Romney was stolen from the Towers last night, Miss, and the whole countryside is up."

"The Romney?" I inquired. "Do you mean a painting?"

"Yes, Miss," he said patiently. "Cut out of its frame, and worth twenty thousand pounds! By a gentlemanly-looking chap—a tourist by appearances, with a bicycle, in tweeds and knickers, Miss."

Whether the bicycle or the tourist wore tweeds and knickers was not entirely clear. Bagsby was saying that the thief was supposed to be hiding on the moor when Daphne came out, and he disappeared.

Poppy Stafford and Ernestine came unexpectedly late that night after I had gone to bed. I was in my first sleep and dreaming that Poppy was braining Bagsby with a gilt-framed painting, and that he was shouting "Votes for Women" instead of "'elp!" when somebody knocked at my door. It turned out to be Poppy, and she said she thought there was a bat in her room, and as she was quite pallid with fright I let her get into my bed. I was full of my dream and I wanted to ask her some particulars about the man she had brained the summer before. But she put her head under the sheet, and as soon as she stopped trembling she went to sleep.

Daphne called me early and we went over to the

Hall to take a look around. As Daphne said, it would be night and the grounds would not matter, but we would have to uncover some of the furniture. And as we could not let the servants know, we had to do it ourselves. We took a brush and pan, and tore up a linen sheet to dust with. Bagsby, who had been bribed, and suspected what he wasn't told, got the brush and pan, and later he showed us a pail and a piece of soap in the tonneau.

The place was dreadful. No doubt the park had been lovely, but it was overshadowed and over-grown. The hedges were untrimmed; paths began, wandered around and died in a mess of under-growth; and the terrace had lost an end in a wilder-ness where a garden-house was falling to decay. The fading outlines of the kitchen garden seemed to shout aloud of lost domesticity, and over every-thing lay a sodden layer of the previous autumn's leaves. (For fear I am accused of plagiarism, the sentence about the kitchen garden is not original. Madge.)

Daphne had got a key somewhere, and inside it was worse. Coverings over the pictures and furni-ture, six years' dust everywhere, and a smell of mould like a crypt of one of the Continental cathe-drals, only not so ancestor-y. While we were tak-ing off the covers, with Bagsby's help, Daphne alternately sang and coughed in the dust.

"Why aren't you more cheerful?" she demanded. "It will be a red-letter day for The Cause. When I think of Mabel Fitzjames I almost weep!"

"I think it must be because I am not used to it," I said meekly. "You see, I come from a Republican country—and Democratic, too, of course—and we don't have any Prime Ministers to steal. One has to grow accustomed to things like this gradually, Daffie, or be born to them. And then—I lay awake most of last night, wondering what would happen if he didn't—er—see the joke, you know."

Daphne jerked a cover from a moth-eaten sofa and sneezed promptly in the dust.

"Joke!" she repeated when she could speak. "No, I don't think he will see the joke. In fact, I don't believe he will think there is any joke to see. If I know anything, he is going to be wild. He's going to tear his hair and throw the vases off the mantel. He's going to use language that you never heard— at least, I hope not."

It was then that I realised that I was not, heart and soul, a Suffragist. If I had only had the courage to have spoken up then, to have told her that I didn't feel The Cause the way I ought to, and that I hoped to get married and have dozens of children, and that, anyhow, I had a headache and I thought I ought to go on to Italy and meet Mother! But, instead, I followed her around like a sheep, tacking up cards with Suffrage mottoes on them all over the drawing-room, and stretching a long canvas banner in the hall across the back of a great Gothic hall-seat, with "Votes for Women" in red letters on it.

Bagsby brushed out a sort of oasis in the middle of the drawing-room and a path to the door, and Daphne and I dusted seven chairs and a table. We had brought over a duplex lamp and some candles, and when we had put a cover on the table the middle of the room looked quite habitable. Then Bagsby brushed the leaves off the steps, and as Daphne pleasantly expressed it:

> *Won't you step into my parlor?*
> *Said the spider to the fly.*

Mrs. Stafford, Violet and Lady Jane arrived that afternoon, after having waited to send the wire on which the conspiracy was hung. They put themselves into negligees and the hands of their maids at once, and were still dressing when Ernestine and I, the advance guard, started with the hamper of cold supper at half after six. Things went wrong from that moment.

Ernestine started to recite her speech to me as we went down the drive, found she had forgotten everything but the first sentence, which began, like The Walrus and the Carpenter, "The time has come——" and had to go back for the manuscript.

We had to leave her for the second trip. Bagsby, who was in the conspiracy to the extent of five pounds, took me over alone and lighted the duplex lamp. He cut the telephone wire, also, by Daphne's order, before he left. We were not leaving anything to chance, although the thing had probably been disconnected for years.

"I 'ardly like to leave you 'ere alone, Miss," he said when everything was ready. It was growing dark by that time and raining again. "Folks is always ready to give a hempty 'ouse a black eye, so to speak. The 'All ghost isn't what you might call authenticated, but the 'ouse isn't 'abitable for a lady alone, Miss."

"I am not at all nervous," I quavered as he went down the steps. "Only—please tell them to hurry, Bagsby."

I called to him again as he climbed into the car.

"Oh, Bagsby," I said nervously, "I—I suppose there is no danger of the picture thief being around."

"Not for pictures, anyhow, Miss," he returned jocularly, and started off.

Not for pictures, anyhow!

I stood at the door and watched the tail light of the motor disappear down the drive, show for an instant a spark by the dilapidated lodge and then go out entirely.

. . . .

The second part of the story begins about here. The first part, as you have seen, has been purely political: the rest is romance, intermingled with crime. It is a little late to bring in a hero, but to have done it earlier would have spoiled the story, besides being distinctly untruthful. And I suppose a real novelist would have had the hero turn out to be the sunburned gentleman of some pages before; but the fact is he wasn't, and I never saw the sunburned gentleman again.

Well, after Bagsby left, and I had examined the supper in the hamper and lighted more candles in the drawing-room, I began to wish we had not cut the telephone wire so soon. It was perfectly dark, and any one could step in through the windows— open to air the house—and cut my throat and take my string of pearls which Father had had matched for me and walk away calmly and be safe ten feet from the house in the undergrowth. And then Bagsby's ghost began to walk in my mind and I quite lost sight of the fact that it was not authenticated.

It was blowing by that time, and every joint of the rheumatic old house creaked and groaned. The candles flickered and nearly went out, and the motto cards began to fly around the room as if carried by invisible fingers. One of them said, "You have been weighed and found wanting," and another one,

"Beware!" They had all the effect of spirit messages on me. When I tried to close the windows I found them stuck in their dilapidated frames. I wanted desperately to hide in a corner behind one of the high-backed chairs, but it was dusty there and hardly dignified for a person who was abducting the Prime Minister. And then it would be ignominious to faint there and have some one peer over the back and say: "Why, here she is!"

So, to divert my mind from ghosts and gentlemen burglars who steal pictures, I began to investigate the hamper. There were *pâté* and salad and sandwiches and quite a lot of stuff. But all at once I remembered that Daphne had given me the small silver and that I had laid it on my bed and left it there. And most of the provisions were too messy for a P. M. to manage with his fingers. Luckily, I remembered something Violet had said when Daphne gave me the silver.

"Personally," she had announced, "I am not in favor of feeding him at all. Or else I would give him prison fare. But if you're going to be mushy over him you'll probably find some dishes and forks in a little closet over the dining-room fire-place. They were kept there to use if Basil ever went down for the shooting, and I dare say they are still there."

So I picked up a candle and trembled through the darkness toward where the breakfast-room ought to be. I went through a square garden-hall which shook when I did, and the motor coat around my shoulders made the shadow of a pirate on the wall.

I found the breakfast-room and the mantel cupboard at last, and, putting the candle on a chair, stood for a moment listening, my hands clapped over my heart. I thought I heard some one walking over bare boards near by, but the sounds, whatever they were, ceased.

The mantel cupboard was locked. I pulled and twisted at the knob to no purpose. Finally, I dug at the lock with a hairpin, and something gave; the door swung open with a squeak, and a moment later I had a flannel case in my hands and was taking out some silver forks. At that moment a plate in the cupboard fell forward with a slam, and something leaped on to the forks, which I dropped with a crash. The candle went out immediately and, gasping for breath, I backed against the cupboard and stood staring into the blackness of the room.

The door by which I had entered was a faint, yellowish rectangle from the distant hall lamp. That is, it had been a rectangle. It was partly obscured now. And gradually the opacity took on the height and breadth and general outline of a man. He was pointing a revolver at me!

III

I think it occurred to him then that I might be pointing something at him—not knowing that my deadliest weapon was a silver fork. For he slid inside the room with his back against the wall. And there we stood, backed against opposite corners, staring into the darkness, and I, for one, totally unable to speak. Finally, he said: "I think it will end right here."

"I—I don't know what you mean," I quavered, for I was plainly expected to say something. There was another total silence, which I learned afterward was inability on *his* part to speak. Then——

"By Jove!" he exclaimed; and then again, under his breath: "By Jove!"

(That assured me somewhat. "By Jove" is so largely a gentleman's exclamation. If he had said "Blow me," which is English lower class, or "Shiver my timbers," I know I should have shivered mine. But "By Jove" gave me courage.)

He fumbled for and lighted a match then, and took a step forward. We had a ghastly glimpse of each other before the match went out, and I saw he was *in tweeds and knickers*, and had one of Daphne's sandwiches in his left hand. He saw the candle then and, stepping forward, he lighted it where it stood on the chair. And when he had lighted it and put it on the table he actually smiled across it.

"I am not sure yet that I am awake," he said easily. "Please don't disappear. The sandwich seems real enough, but that's the way in dreams. You find something delectable and wake up before you taste it. You see, the sandwich is gone already."

"You dropped it," I said as calmly as I could.

"Oh," he said, lowering the candle and peering under the table. "Ah, here it is. So it isn't a dream! You have no idea how many times I have dreamed I was finding money—sovereigns, you know, and all that—and wakened at the psychological moment." He put his revolver on the table, took a bite of the sandwich and stared at me, at my gown, *and then at my pearls.* I fancied his eyes gleamed.

I did not speak; I was listening with all my might for the car, but I could hear nothing but the patter of the rain on the flagstones outside.

"I'm afraid I have startled you," he went on, still looking at me with uncomfortable intentness. "The fact is, I was asleep. I got in through a window an hour or so ago after a day and a night on the moor. I had no idea there was anybody here until you brushed past me in the dark."

The moor! Then of course I knew. It had been dawning on me slowly. For all I could tell, he might have had the Romney under his coat at that moment. I put my hands to my throat for air because, although he was smiling and pleasant enough, everybody knows that the bigger the game a burglar makes a specialty of the more likely he·is to look and act like a gentleman. So, because he seemed to expect me to do something, I unclasped my collar with shaking fingers and threw it to him across the table.

"Oh, please take it and go away," I implored him. "It—it isn't imitation, anyhow, and Daphne says—the Romney was."

"Oh," he said slowly, staring at the pearls, "so Daphne says the Romney was, eh?"

He ran the collar through his fingers as if his conscience was troubling him a little. Then, "I wouldn't care to pit my judgment against that of a lady," he went on without even a word about the collar, "but —I think your friend Daphne is wrong." His eyes travelled comprehensively to the silver on the floor.

"If you don't mind," he said whimsically—(this seems the only word, although—can a burglar be whimsical?)—"I wish you would tell me how you opened that cupboard door. It was locked an hour ago."

"I dare say it was very unprofessional," I said boldly—for he didn't show any sign of trying to choke me, and my courage was returning, "but—I did it with a hairpin."

"Ah!" He was thoughtful. "And—I suppose that is the way you opened the front entry door, also?"

"No. Violet had a key——" I began. Then I stopped, furious at myself.

He dropped the sandwich again and took a step forward with his eyes narrowed.

"Violet!" he said.

It seems extraordinary, looking back, to think I could have mistaken him for a theif when he was something else altogether. But that wasn't the only mistake I made. I could scream when I remember He was not at all like his picture, and because I hadn't recognised him as Basil Harcourt, who hated The Cause, I had lost quantities of valuable time.

One thinks quickly in emergencies, and women have one advantage over men. They can think very hard while they are talking about an entirely dif‹ ferent subject. His next question gave me a cue. He came forward and leaned on the table, near the candle. I could see he was not very old after all— not nearly so old as I had expected.

"I know it isn't my affair at all," he began, half smiling, "but—I am under the impression that the Hall has been closed for some years. And yet—I find a young woman here alone, surrounded by—

er—dust and decay. It's a sort of reversed Sleeping Beauty and the Prince. *You* should have been asleep. As you say, it isn't my affair, but—what in the world brought you here?"

(When I told this afterward Poppy said: "It sounds exactly like him, of course.")

"I came to steal the silver," I said brazenly.

That was my plan, you see. If he would only take me away and give me in charge he would be safely out of the way and beyond interfering. And the next morning, when everything was over, I would tell my real name and be released, and everything would be over. Something had to be done at once, for, as Daphne said, "to kidnap the Prime Minister would be a *coup d'état*, but to try to do it and fail would be low comedy."

When I said I was stealing the silver, which was certainly not worth five guineas, Mr. Harcourt took a step back and caught hold of a chair.

"Really!" he said. And then: "But what in the world did you intend doing with it?—if you don't mind the question."

This was unexpected, but I rose to the occasion.

"Melt it," I declared. I thought this was inspired. Don't they always melt down stolen silver?

"By Jove!" he exclaimed. "You *are* experienced!" Then he sat down suddenly in the chair and coughed very hard into his handkerchief. But he made no move to arrest me.

"Aren't you going to give me in charge?" I asked in alarm, for time was flying. He put away his handkerchief.

"Wouldn't that be a horrible thing for me to do?" he asked gravely. "Perhaps it's your first offence, you know, although I doubt that. You seem so capable And if I let you go you may reform. Take my word for it, there's nothing to a life of crime I suppose you—er—appropriated the string of pearls that are not imitation?"

This was unexpected.

"It is mine, honestly mine, Mr. Harcourt," I began. He glanced at me when I called him by name. Then he took the collar out and looked at it. "I shall advertise it," he said judicially and slid it back into his pocket. "If the owner offers a reward I will see that you get it—minus the newspaper costs, of course."

Then—we both heard it at the same moment—there came the throb of the machine down the drive. He raised his eyebrows and glanced at me. "More people after the silver, probably," he said, and picked up the candle. I slipped after him to the entrance hall.

Just inside the door, with a cordial smile of greeting fading into a blank, stood a middle-aged English gentleman, rather florid, with a drooping, sandy moustache and thinnish hair. When he saw me the ghost of the smile returned.

"I am sure I beg your pardon. A—a thousand apologies. That cursed—hem—the chauffeur has made a beastly mistake. I was led to believe—I— that is——"

He was staring at me. Then his eye struck the banner across the hall, with "Votes for Women" on it, and from there it travelled to Mr. Harcourt. He had grown visibly paler. He put a hand to his tweed travelling-cap, gave it a jerk and, turning without warning, he disappeared through the entry into the storm. I caught Mr. Harcourt by the arm as he was about to follow, muttering savagely.

"Oh, he's going to run away," I wailed. "And he will take pneumonia or something like that, and die! I told Daphne how it would be!" Mr. Harcourt ran down the steps. "Sir George! Sir George!" I called desperately into the darkness from the doorway. There was no answer, but Mr. Harcourt stopped and glanced back from the drive.

"Sir George!" he exclaimed. "What do you mean?"

"It's the Prime Minister," I called desperately, "and if you care anything at all about Violet—but, of course, you don't—oh, do find him and bring him back!"

(Nothing but the excitement of the occasion would have made me mention Violet to him. I was sorry on the instant, for Mother knew a man once who had a fainting spell every time he heard his divorced wife's name, and the only way they could revive him was by sprinkling him with lilac water, which had been her favourite perfume. Very romantic, I think. But there was nothing but rain to sprinkle on Mr. Harcourt, even if he had taken a fit, which he didn't.)

Instead, he turned on his heel and started down the drive. Sir George had disappeared, and the engine of the motor car had given a final throb and died in the distance. Sounds of feet splashing through mud and water came back to me.

For ten minutes I cowered on that miserable settee, with "Votes for Women" over my head. And I remembered America, and the way I was always sheltered there, and nobody even thinking of kidnapping the Cabinet. The President being the whole thing anyhow and always guarded by secret service men. And besides, imagine abducting nine men! Or is it seven?

After eternities I heard voices outside and Mr. Harcourt appeared, half leading, half coaxing Sir George. He had him by the arm. The Prime Minister was oozing mud and he was very pale.

"Terrible!" he was saying. "Unbelievable! Is

there anything they won't do!" Then he caught a glimpse of the seven chairs and the gavel on the drawing-room table, and tried to bolt again. But the entry door was closed.

"Now, then," Mr. Harcourt said to me disagreeably. "Tell us what you know about this thing. It isn't an accident, I presume?"

I shook my head.

"You see, sir," he said to the P. M., "you are the centre—the storm centre—of a Suffragette plot of some sort. I was a fool not to have guessed it, but I actually thought—— Well, no matter what I thought. I presume you were going to Gresham Place?"

Sir George nodded and groaned. A terrible flash of lightning was followed almost instantly by a splintering crash. The very house rocked. Mr. Harcourt closed the door.

"This is Harcourt Hall," he explained. "It's in bad shape, but we have at least a roof. I think you are alone?" to me very curtly.

I nodded mutely.

"I fancy the best thing under the circumstances is to wire to Gresham Place, and have them send a car over—providing the telephone is in order."

"The wire is cut," I broke in. And then, like the poor thing I am, I began to cry. I hate lightning. It always makes me nervous.

Both Sir George and Mr. Harcourt stared at me helplessly. And then, still sniffling, I told them the whole story, and how Daphne and the rest would soon be there, and that I wasn't really a Suffragette; that I was an American, and I thought women ought to vote, but be ladylike and proper about it, and that, at least, they ought to be school directors, because they understood little children so well and paid taxes, anyhow.

When I got through and looked up at them Sir George was staring at me in bewilderment and Mr. Harcourt was smiling broadly.

"My dear young lady," he said, "of course you ought to vote. And if voting went by general attractiveness you would have to be what Americans call a repeater—vote twice, you know."

(It was at this point, when I told the story, that Ernestine Sutcliffe looked contemptuous. "We are not *all* pretty puppets," she said. And I retorted: "No, I should say not!")

All this had taken longer than it sounds, for on the very tail of Mr. Harcourt's speech came a double honk from the drive. Mr. Harcourt jumped for the hall lamp and extinguished it in an instant. I hardly know what happened next. My eyes were still staring wide into the blackness when he reached over and clutched me by the shoulder.

"Not a word, please," he ordered. "This way,

Sir George! The door is bolted, and we will have time to get upstairs and hide. There's a secret room, if I can remember how to get to it. Walk lightly."

I could hear Daphne at the door outside and I opened my mouth to scream. But Mr. Harcourt divined my intention and clapped a hand over it.

As I was half led, half dragged back through the dark hall I saw Violet enter by one of the windows.

IV

We got upstairs somehow, with Sir George breathing in gasps. I realised then that Mr. Harcourt was still supporting me and I freed myself with a jerk, on which he coolly took my hand and led the way along the musty hall. Once or twice boards creaked and the two men stopped in alarm. But no one heard. From below came a babel of high, excited voices and the crash of an overturned chair. I backed against the wall and held my hands out defensively in front of me.

"How dare you carry me off like this!" I demanded when I could speak. "I am going back!"

But Mr. Harcourt blocked the passage with his broad shoulders and struck a match cautiously. First he looked at the walls, then he glanced at me.

"My dear young lady," he said curtly, "we should be only too happy to leave you—but you know

too much." Then, to Sir George: "I must have taken
a wrong turn," he whispered ruefully. "There ought
to be a wainscoting here. Good Heavens! I believe they are coming up."

We could hear Daphne calling "Madge!"
frantically from the lower stairs. And suddenly I
was ashamed of the whole affair: of myself, for
lending myself to it; of Violet, for thrusting the man
beside me out of her life and then stooping to borrow his house; of Poppy, for braining a man with
a chair and then being afraid of a bat. I turned to
Mr. Harcourt as the footsteps ran up the stairs.

"The door at the end of the corridor is partly
open," I whispered. "We may be able to lock it
behind us."

With that *we* I shifted my allegiance. From that
moment my sole object was to get the Prime Minister of Great Britain back to his family, his friends
and his Sovereign without injury.

We scurried down the hall and closed the door behind us. It did not lock! But there was no time to
go elsewhere. We stood just inside the door, breathing hard, and listened. For a time the search con-
fined itself to the lower floor. Mr. Harcourt struck
another match and looked around him.

We were in a huge, old-fashioned bedroom with
mullioned windows and panelled walls. The furni-
ture was carefully covered, and the carpet had been

folded and wrapped in the centre of the floor. I sat down on it in a perfectly exhausted condition.

Mr. Harcourt stood with his back against the door and we all listened. But the search had not penetrated to our wing. Sir George was breathing heavily and mopping his head. The air was stiffling.

"I'm awfully sorry," said Mr. Harcourt cautiously; "I could have sworn I had taken the right turn. If I remember rightly there was a passage from the Refuge Chamber down to the garden. How many women are downstairs?"

"Six," I whispered, "and I suppose Poppy Stafford would count as two. She almost killed a man last year." When Sir George heard Poppy's name he began to fumble with the window-lock. "And, of course," I went on, "your—I mean—Violet knows the house perfectly."

"If we could get out of here," Mr. Harcourt reflected, "we could get down to the lodge somehow. Then, when the motor comes back we could stop it at the gates—have them closed, you know—and when the chauffeur gets out to open them steal the car."

Sir George relaxed perceptibly. "A valuable suggestion," he said almost cheerfully. But suddenly I had turned cold.

"Most valuable," I said from the darkness, "save

for one thing: Mr. Harcourt has forgotten, no doubt, but there are no gates at the lodge!"

He gave a quick movement in the darkness. "Then we will have to manage without gates," he said quite calmly. "I had forgotten, for the moment, that they had been taken down. What's the conundrum? When is a gate not a gate?"

But his lightness did not reassure me. Why had he taken the wrong turning in his own house? And what man in his senses would forget whether his own lodge had gates or not! But there was no time to puzzle it out. The search had abandoned the first floor and was coming up the stairs. The Prime Minister threw open the window. From down the hall came a babel of voices and Daphne's soap-box and monument voice. "I think I had better tell you," she was saying "that Violet and I have found traces of two men—muddy footprints that lead up the stairs. Bagsby says he brought Sir George alone. I do not hazard a guess, but—something unforeseen has happened. I only hope——" Here she broke off, and there was a rattle of metallic objects that sounded like brass fire-irons.

The search came our way slowly but certainly. I sat on my carpet and shivered. Mr. Harcourt stood braced against the door, and Sir George had got the window open and was testing the roof of a conservatory with his foot. Footsteps came down the hall and we sat motionless. I remembered suddenly that somebody always sneezed at crises like these, and then I realised inevitably that I was going to be the person. Somewhere I had heard that if you hold your breath and swallow at the psychological moment you may sneeze silently. So I tried it in desperation and almost strangled, and felt very queer about the ears for an hour after. And at the best there was some sound, for the footsteps outside turned and ran toward the stairs, where there was a hurried colloquy.

At that, Sir George put the other foot over the windowsill, and in a moment we were all in headlong flight. Luckily, the very top of the conservatory was boarded on top of the glass, but it began to slope sooner than I had expected, and I lost my hold on Sir George's hand and slid without warning. I landed on the ground below, standing up to my waist in shrubbery and very much jarred. Sir George was not so lucky. He put a foot through a pane of glass with a terrible crash, and it took all of Mr. Harcourt's strength to release him. Standing below, I could see a flare of light in the room we had just left, and the silhouettes of the two men struggling on the roof. Somebody came to the window just as we were united on the soggy ground. I think it was Violet, but the crash of the rain on the glass of the conservatory had covered the noise of our escape.

Mr. Harcourt picked me out of my bush and we darted into the shrubbery.

V

I have only a sketchy recollection of what followed. The rain beat on my face and my bare shoulders; the drive was a river. Once some one came to the entry door of the Hall behind us and waved a lamp, which the wind promptly extinguished. And on either side of me, in gloomy silence, ploughed the Prime Minister and Mr. Harcourt. Once Sir George left the drive, seeking better walking on the turf, and came back after a moment with a brief statement that he had collided with a tree and had loosened a tooth. And twice Mr. Harcourt touched my elbow to guide me and I shook him off.

He got into the gatekeeper's house through a window and opened the door for us. The interior was desolate enough, but it was at least dry. Mr. Harcourt produced a candle from his pocket, evidently from the room we had left, and it revealed two packing-cases, one small keg, and a collection of straw and rubbish in a corner. It also showed that Sir George had struck his nose and that it was bleeding profusely. I got a glimpse, too, of the wreck of my gown, and that and the blood together brought

my responsibility for the whole thing home to me.
I sat down on the keg and buried my face in my
hands.

When I looked up again a fire was crackling on
the hearth and Sir George's boots were steaming in
front of it. Mr. Harcourt had taken off his coat
and was drying it. The smell of wet woollen cloth
filled the air. He smiled at me over his shoulder.

"This is for you," he said cheerfully. "Go into
the back room and strip off that draggled gown and
put this on."

"I'm very well as I am," I said, and shivered.

"Nonsense!" He came over to me and held out
the coat. "That white satin is saturated. Don't be
idiotic. This is certainly no time to stand on
propriety."

"I—I can't," I stammered.

"Now, look here," he persisted. "I've got sisters
—lots of 'em, and Sir George is a grandfather. Put
this on over your petticoat."

Now, of course, anybody who knows anything
about clothing today knows that petticoats don't belong with it. And even if they did, there were about
eighty-seven hooks on the back of my gown, and only
four that I could reach.

"I am very comfortable as I am," I said stubbornly. "Please don't bother about me. I sha'n't
make any change."

He flung the coat angrily on to a box and turned his back squarely on me. It was maddening to have him think me some prudish little schoolgirl who would say limbs for legs, and who, after showing them for years in very short frocks, suddenly puts on her first long gown and is for denying she has any limbs—that is, legs. Sir George sneezed and drew a long, shuddering breath.

"Terrible!" he said. "This is what comes of admitting women to the universities. Would any man in his senses believe that such a situation as this is real?"

Nobody answered. Sir George was inspecting the inner room. I had gone to the window, and after a moment Mr. Harcourt joined me there. The thunder, which had ceased, was commencing again, and a blue-white flash threw out the landscape. It showed a long stretch of country road, running with mad little streams of yellow water, the drive curving past and flowing a dignified tributary into the lane, and it revealed something else. *The lodge gates were there, opened back against the shrubbery!* Under cover of the noise I turned to my companion.

"Who are you?" I demanded under my breath. "You are not Basil Harcourt! You had no more right to be in that house than I had."

"Save the right of sanctuary," he returned, looking at me oddly. "I got in through the chapel.

And what does it matter, anyhow? It is enough for me just now that you are you and I am I."

"You are flippant," I retorted cautiously. "Why did you say you had had the gates taken down when they are still there, opened against the hedge?"

"Jove! That's a piece of luck," he exclaimed, without troubling to explain. "Why in the world did you say there were no gates?"

He opened the door and ran out into the storm. A moment later I saw him testing the hinges, and I flung away from the window. Before he came back he had closed the outer shutters.

Sir George had taken off his mackintosh and cap and, with a candle and a deck of cards, was preparing for solitaire on the top of the keg. The candle-light struck full on his face and showed his sandy moustache hanging limp and dejected, while little beads of moisture showed between the thin hair brushed across the top of his head. He was more nervous than he would have had us know, and the hands—very fine, long-fingered hands they were —that laid out the cards were trembling noticeably. At every sound he raised his head and stared at the door, and his arched, patrician nose would have been pinched if it had not been so swollen. I shuddered with remorse every time I looked at him. His right trouser was torn to ribbons from the knee down, and soon after our arrival he had disappeared into the rear room and emerged, bandaged with his spare handkerchiefs, and limping.

We sat there for two hours, Sir George pretending to play, I huddled on a box by the fire, and The Unknown across the hearth from me, stretched on the floor, and leaning on his elbows and whistling softly. Sometimes he looked at me and sometimes at the fire, and once or twice I found him watching Sir George with a curiously meditative gaze. I could not help wondering if he was thinking what a chance for ransom there would be if he could hold the two of us prisoner for a time.

(For story purposes, it is a pity he did not. What a novel it would have made! The whole House of Lords out searching for us, and the Premier and myself living in a cave, with our captor sitting at the entrance with a gun across his knees!)

After two hours of cards and steaming before the fire Sir George became drowsy. He yawned prodigiously, apologised to me thickly, and when the candle finally burned out he put his head on top of the keg and was asleep immediately. Not a sound had come from the Hall; everything was quiet except for a drip from the leaking roof, that splashed in a corner.

Then:

"If you please," I said in a small voice, "may I have my necklace now?"

The Unknown turned quickly and glanced at Sir

George, but he was noisily asleep. Then he edged over along the hearth until he was almost at my feet.

"I was going to advertise them," he said in an undertone. "Possibly you recall my fair offer. Some poor woman is probably having a serious illness at this minute because her pearls have been— er—appropriated."

"I don't feel a particle ill," I said stubbornly, "but I want them back. They belong to me. What are you going to do with them?"

" 'Melt them down and sell them,' " he quoted easily. "Or dissolve them in vinegar and swallow them. That's historic, anyhow."

"There is a better Biblical precedent," I said and stopped, furious at myself. He was an ordinary highwayman masquerading as a gentleman, and for all I knew he might at that very minute have had the stolen Romney sewed around him like a cuirass. (He *did* hold himself very erect, now I thought of it.) And I had allowed his debonair manner to carry me away.

But he did not give me a chance to snub him, for the next moment he was speaking gravely in an undertone and looking directly in my eyes. I will say he had a most misleadingly frank expression.

"I will give them to you when you are safely back at Ivry," he said, "and not one moment before.

I am sure Sir George would agree with me that they are too valuable for a young girl to wear under the circumstances. I will give you my word, if it is worth anything to you."

"And if I will not take it?"

"It would make no difference," he replied imperturbably, and leaned over to replenish the fire.

Sir George slept on noisily; the drip in the corner had become a splash; my white satin slippers before the fire were drying into limp shapelessness. The man in tweeds on the floor raised himself into a sitting position and listened, his hands clasped about his knees.

(Knickers with a man are like *décolletage* with a woman, only to be worn by the elect. Mother wishes me to cut this out, because she says this story is to be read by young persons. But the modern young person is really awfully sophisticated. Sometimes I feel as though mother is a mere child, compared to me.)

After a time the man in knickers who was one of the elect dropped on his elbow and began to talk again, looking into the fire.

"Rum affair altogether, isn't it?" he said chattily. "Nature having a spasm outside, half a dozen lady votaries of the vote having spasms up at the house, the—er—Premier of Great Britain, on whose possessions the sun never sets, having apoplexy on a packing-case. And out of all this chaos a moment like this: you and I alone here, where I could reach out my hand and touch you—if I dared——" he supplemented as I straightened. "You see, you have gone to my head. You are the most beautiful person I have ever seen."

One could tell that, however low he had fallen, he had been properly raised—although I think firelight is always becoming, especially with a white gown.

Here Sir George began to rouse. He coughed huskily, sat up and looked around him in a daze, and then stretched out his legs and groaned.

"Gad!" he said with a deep breath, "I hoped I had dreamed it." He looked at us both as if to establish our reality, and, reaching over, began to struggle into his shrunken boots.

"If the storm has subsided," he said, stamping his foot in an endeavour to get his heel down where it belonged, "I think I shall be going on. This place is damp."

"Not half so damp as the road," objected the other man. "It's a matter of miles, you know; and besides, I imagine we are going to have another storm. Listen!"

The distant rumble of thunder had been coming closer to us. The rain had almost stopped, but, as Sir George opened the door, over the ominous stillness flashed a terrific fork of lightning, followed instantly by a crash near at hand. A blue-white streak ran down the bole of a tree across the road. The thunder that followed echoed and re-echoed above our heads as we faced each other in the firelight. Sir George had closed the door precipitately, but, as the noise died away, he jammed his cap over his ears and resolutely prepared for flight.

Argument had no effect on him. Whatever had caused his sudden change of mind, he was determined to leave at once. I was panic-stricken. He had been my patent of respectability so far in what was, to say the least, an unconventional situation. But to have him go like that and leave me there with an ordinary thief, even if he did look like a Greek god except his nose, which was modern—(I do not like those old Greek noses, anyhow; they begin so far up on the forehead)—to have him leave me like that was dreadful.

However, there came an interruption just then, a splashing of horses' feet along the road and the sound of men's voices. They halted just outside the gates and we caught a word here and there: "Gresham Place," and "Automobile," and one sentence that stuck in my mind and brought me a picture of myself in a hideous prison cap, sewing bags. It was: "Half a dozen are watching Ivry Manor House!"

I think Sir George realised when I did that it was a searching party for him; he had been leaning against the door, listening. Suddenly he bolted for the keg where he had left his mackintosh, and picked it up. But The Unknown was before him. He quickly locked the outer door and stood with his back against it.

"I cannot allow you to go out, sir," he said very politely. "Whether those men are searching for you or are hunting for—for some one else, you and I have a duty to perform: we must protect this young lady. In fact, and however strongly you may feel against it, I hope, sir, you will see the wisdom of shielding all the women concerned from publicity. And in this case it is not chivalry; it is self-protection." Sir George wavered. "You can see what the papers will make of it, sir. That the plot has failed would not check the general excitement; the situation is ludicrous instead of serious. That is the difference."

Sir George sat down heavily and groaned. Perhaps I imagined it, but he looked older, leaner, paler than he had done earlier in the evening.

"I have this plan to offer," pursued The Unknown. "We will get the machine from Bagsby in an hour"— he consulted a handsome watch; I wondered whose it had been—"and I will take you wherever you wish; to Gresham Place, or, if you will feel safer back in town, to the express for London. You can get it at East Newbury. If—if the young lady wishes, we will drop her at Ivry on the way."

Sir George considered and decided to go back to town. He would not feel safe, after this, in the country, and he could wire ahead and be met by— I think he said he intended to call out the reserves. I may be wrong about this, but he gave me the impression that he would never walk out again without a detachment of the Royal Guard.

And so we settled down again to wait for Bagsby —that is, we settled down apparently; actually, I was busy devising a method to get rid of our highwayman and to secure my necklace again. For any one could tell that he only meant to get Daphne's motor to escape in and that he would probably dump Sir George and me in a ditch, or cut our throats, or sandbag us, and make his escape with everything valuable on us, including my slipper buckles which were platinum and had my monogram on in diamonds.

If I could only have warned Sir George! But there The Unknown sat between us, with his eyes on both of us at once (if this is possible in anything but a fish), asking me how I liked England and what I thought of wealthy American girls marrying impoverished foreigners; and did I know that in the Canadian Northwest Mounted Police the word "home" was practically taboo! And I said I abominated England and that I couldn't understand any kind of an American girl marrying any Englishman, and where was Canada? He gave up at that and, producing a gold cigarette-case with somebody's initials on it, smoked moodily for some time.

Then I had my second inspiration of the evening. I began to get hungry, and by stages I grew weak, dizzy and, finally, almost fainting. Sir George was very mildly interested, but The Unknown was flatteringly so. However, when I said faintly that I had had no dinner, and that I was sure I should swoon if I did not have the hamper brought from the Hall at once, he cooled somewhat.

"You would better try to stick it out," he urged. "You haven't had any dinner: I haven't had food for—well, for some time. There's a tap in the back room: let me bring you a drink of water. You have no idea, until you have to, how long you can go on water."

"I am not a boat," I said scornfully. And after a time, when he proved shockingly distrustful of me and most unchivalrous, he agreed grudgingly to try to steal the hamper from the house.

"But remember," he said, turning up his coat collar, "if anything goes wrong you will have the whole shooting-match down on us here." (Item: was he

American, after all? An Englishman would have said "the whole bally crowd.")

I think he wanted to say something to me before he left, but having gained my point I turned my back on him. He went, finally, but he stood for a moment on the lodge porch, looking back at me. I pretended not to know it.

When I heard him splashing up the drive I turned on Sir George like a hurricane. It took him some time to understand; I had to go over the part about the pearls several times, and when he finally made out that they were very valuable he still could not understand how I came to throw them at the other man. Then I told him about the theft of the picture, and that we had the thief in our grasp if we could get him. Sir George's face was very queer. When he got it all finally, however, he wakened up at once. He asked me what the collar was worth, and said young English girls did not wear such costly jewels, but that he would see that they were recovered. And the plan was simple enough. The greatest things in life are simple. I said to him that I could easily see how he became Premier.

The shutters of the inner room were bolted on the outside. We would coax our gentleman in there and lock the door. He would be there, as I said with enthusiasm to Sir George, like a ripe apple on a tree, ready for picking at any time.

It worked to a charm, although the result was not what we had expected. Very far from it, indeed. The Unknown, which is shorter than saying "The Man in Tweeds" or "The Sociable Highwayman," came back in about half an hour, with his cap missing and mud up to his knees.

"Jove," he said, shaking himself, "this is Paradise compared to that up there. The lower floor is a wreck: two of them are asleep, three of them are standing on chairs and talking at once, and a tall, fair woman in green satin is having ladylike hysterics by herself in a corner."

"The tall, fair woman in green," I said coldly, "is Mrs. Harcourt-Standish. It is strange you did not know her."

He whistled and then looked at me with one of his slow, boyish smiles.

"Well, as to that," he observed, opening the hamper, "I—you see, I never saw her in hysterics. It's supposed to make a great difference."

"We need a box from the other room," I said, inwardly trembling. "We have used one for firewood." We had, purposely, and it threatened to fire the chimney. I don't mind saying that I had a horrid guilty feeling when I said it, like Delilah cutting Samson's hair, or the place where Blanche Bates took the card out of her stocking in The Girl of the Golden West. The Unknown glanced at the box on the hearth, at the Prime Minister, who was getting out the salad, and at me, feeling as I have just said. Then he turned on his heel, whistling softly, and went into the inner room.

Sir George dropped the salad on the instant, with a crash, and had the door slammed and locked immediately. His sandy moustache stood out quite straight, and he looked very military (or is it militant?). There was silence from the inner room, and then my gentleman found the door and rattled the crazy latch.

"The lock has sprung in some way," he said politely from the other side. "I will have to trouble you to open it."

The band around my throat began to loosen, and, anyhow, if he had been little and ugly I would not have cared. Why should I condone a crime because Nature had given him a handsome body to hold an ignoble spirit? I went over to the door and called through it triumphantly:

"We are not going to unlock the door, and when Bagsby comes we are going to send for the police."

(That was the Premier's plan. He would waylay Bagsby at the point of his revolver—Sir George's—and make him take him to the nearest constable. Then Sir George would get a conveyance and make his escape after sending me on to Ivry. I would not stay in the lodge alone with a desperate criminal, and I did not wish to face Daphne and the rest in their present condition.)

I was not hungry, after all. Everything I ate stuck somewhere in my throat and brought tears to my eyes, and Sir George was not hungry, either. He kept walking around the room and eying the door, and once he got out his revolver and put it on the box. Finally, he went to the doorway.

"If you will pass this young woman's jewelry out under the door," he said, "we will see that you are not molested by the police."

"On our honour!" I called eagerly. For, after all, he had been gentle with me when he thought I was stealing the forks. (Although, after all, why should he not have been? They were not his.)

"I'll see you in perdition first!" came the sulky answer. I hoped it was meant for Sir George. And after that there was nothing to do but wait for Bagsby.

VI

We did not talk. Sir George watched the door to the inner room and sneezed frequently. Part of the time he examined his revolver, which he put on the keg in front of him. He was very clumsy with it; I suppose a Prime Minister has an armour-bearer usually, or something of that sort. Once we heard an automobile far off, and Sir George ran out to the gates and closed them. But the machine went past, and from the voices it seemed to be filled with men. I saw it again later.

While Sir George was outside in the rain I emptied his revolver. It is one thing to have a man arrested for stealing one's jewels, and quite a different one to murder him in cold blood. I had the cartridges in my hand when Sir George opened the door, and in my excitement I threw them into the fire. From that moment until we left I stood behind one of the packing-cases and waited for the hearth to open fire on us. But for some reason the cartridges did not explode. Perhaps they fell too far back in the chimney.

(I. E. This would make a good plot for a detective story. Some time I shall try it. Writing is much easier than I had thought it would be, especially conversation. The villain could put a row of shells on a fire-log, pointing toward the hero's easy-chair. The hero comes home and lights the fire, and then the heroine, whom the villain loves, comes on some agonised errand to the hero's room at night, sits in his chair and is murdered. Of course, the hero is suspected, or perhaps the villain jumps from behind a curtain to save the lady, kneels on the hearth-rug and gets a broadside that finishes him. You can see the possibilities.)

Sir George was growing distinctly less agreeable.

He made another appeal to the prisoner to give up the necklace and put it out under the door, but the prisoner did not make any reply.

At three o'clock Bagsby came. We hurried out to the little porch and watched him stop the car just beside us, with its nose at the gates. As he was getting out, muttering, to open them, Sir George caught him by the shoulder and held the revolver under his nose.

"Get back into the car," he commanded, "and take this young woman and myself to Newbury. And mind you do it. No nonsense. Do you know the road?"

Bagsby muttered sullenly that he did, and then, just when I was safely in the tonneau and had drawn a long breath, Sir George stopped with his foot on the step and—I think he swore. Then he put the revolver in my hand and pointed it at Bagsby's neck.

"Do you know how to shoot?" he demanded.

"Ye—yes."

"I have forgotten my mackintosh," he explained curtly. "Shoot him if he attempts to start the car." He turned in the doorway to say: "Don't take your finger off the trigger." I might just as well have been pointing the automobile wrench, for there was nothing in the revolver.

Then he went into the cottage, and was gone fully

a minute. But the strange thing was that as he went into the house a lightning flash lit up his figure, and he had his mackintosh over his arm! However, he might have meant his goloshes, which is English for overshoes and sounds like mackintosh. (I know at home I always confuse Wabash and Oshkosh.) While he was in the house the second strange thing happened. Bagsby squirmed in his seat in front of me and said in a muffled voice: "Be easy with that trigger, Miss!"

It was not Bagsby at all! *It was the prisoner we had locked in the inner room!*

"Oh!" I said limply, and the revolver slid out of my lap. He turned cautiously and bent over the back of the driver's seat.

"Everything's all right," he said quickly. "You are perfectly safe; I am going to take you home. Unload that revolver, won't you, before he gets back? Or let me do it."

"It *is* unloaded," I quavered. "I did it myself. But why——?"

"Sh! Hold out your hand."

I did, slowly, and I felt my necklace drop into it. He caught my fingers and held them.

"Now, will you trust me?" he whispered. We could hear Sir George falling over boxes in the house and talking to himself. "I have been fair with *you*, haven't I?"

"I—yes!" I couldn't say less, could I, with the pearls in my hand? "I—I suppose I can trust you. I only want to go home and have a cup of weak tea and go to bed."

"Good girl!" he said. "Of course you can trust me." And leaning over, without any warning, he kissed my palm, while the necklace slid to the floor of the tonneau beside the revolver. It was all most amazing. "Not a word to Sir George, please. He is upset enough as it is. It is my turn to trust you."

"But I don't understand," I was beginning, when Sir George came to the door of the cottage. At that moment one of the cartridges in the fire exploded, and without looking back he leaped off the porch and into the car. I had only time to pick up the revolver and to point its harmless barrel at the chauffeur's back. I have no doubt that to this minute Sir George thinks that a desperate attempt was made that night on his life. For reasons that I am coming to, I never explained. I am very vague about the next thirty minutes. We passed a man, I recall, some distance down the lane, a man who turned and yelled at us through the storm, and I rather thought that it was Bagsby. I couldn't be quite certain. And after we had gone perhaps a mile we met the automobile we had heard earlier coming back through the mud. We made a détour which almost ditched us, and passed them without slackening speed.

The pace was terrific. Sir George and I rattled about in the tonneau, now jammed together at one side and now at another. I was much too busy trying to stay in the car to have time to wonder what it all meant. But I found out soon enough.

The other car had turned and was following us! It was coming very fast, too; and they had taken off the muffler, which made it even more alarming. When Sir George saw that we were being pursued he became frantic. After threatening the supposed Bagsby he began to offer bribes. For, of course, one could understand that the position was an ignominious one for any Prime Minister, and that his dignity would be sure to suffer if we were overtaken and the story came out. How many times at home I have sat in a theatre and seen cinematograph pictures of people in a motor being followed at top speed, with perhaps an angry father shaking his fist from the pursuing car. But never had I expected to be playing castanets with the Premier of Great Britain in the tonneau of a machine driven by a highwayman, and flying from unknown pursuers who were chasing us for Heaven knows what reason. Even at the time I remember thinking what a cinematograph picture we would make.

Up to this point the story has been mild enough.

Now it becomes tragic. For at the place where the car should have kept straight on to go to Newbury it turned suddenly, putting me in Sir George's lap for a moment, and jounced along over mud and ruts, through a narrow lane. Sir George threw me off ungallantly and yelled. Then he leaned over and held the revolver against the driver's neck.

"What do you mean?" he almost shrieked. "Where are you going, sir? This is not the road to Newbury!" But the car kept on. Sir George was frantic. He demanded that the car be stopped, so he could get out and hide in the hedge. He snapped the trigger, regardless of the fact that had it been loaded we would have gone crashing into eternity and a tree at forty miles an hour.

Then he commanded our chauffeur to turn around and ram the pursuing car to destruction, although he put it differently. And then, finding he made no impression on the hooded and goggled figure in the driver's seat, he stood up frantically and poised the revolver to brain the man at the wheel.

He was quite mad. It was not courage on my part that made me leap and catch his arm. It was sheer self-preservation. The revolver hurtled into the road. (I cannot find the dictionary, but I'm sure "hurtled" is correct, and certainly it is forceful. The revolver hurtled into the road, and Sir George collapsed, with me on top of him. Afterwards, of course, I had chills, because, being the Prime Minister, no doubt he could have me put in the Tower or beheaded, or something dreadful. And would it be "lèse-majesté" to knock over the King's representative?

By this time we were well up the lane, and the other car shot past along the highroad. But our pace did not moderate, and after a little the other car found its mistake and came back. We could hear it a quarter of a mile or so behind us. And at that precise instant we began to slow up: the engine struggled for a few yards, began to pant, gave two or three exhausted gasps, and then turned over on its side and died. The next moment we were all three in the road and running like mad up a hill.

If one knows *where* one is going, and whom one is with, and who is behind one shouting "Stop thief!" it is not so bad. But to have a man you don't know take you by the arm and drag you along through briers and mud toward Heaven knows where, with half a dozen other men just below climbing faster than you can run, and it is raining, and you haven't an idea what it is all about—well, it is not pleasant. And I had lost a heel off one slipper and was three inches shorter on one side than on the other.

Sir George was for refusing the hill and for dodging among the trees, but our deliverer (?) held him tight. Once, in a frenzy of alarm, he did break loose, but he was promptly captured and brought back, with apologies, but firmness. It was easy to see why. He would have caught his death of cold if he had wandered over those hills all night in the rain, and what would have become of England? (I am very glad there are no Prime Ministers in America, and most of the Presidents that I recall would be as easy to run away with as a bull hippopotamus.)

And then we found ourselves at a side entry of what seemed to be a colossal house. The door was partly open and a man in livery was asleep on a bench just inside the door.

The hold on my arm was released. The Prime Minister, assisted by The Unknown, went up the steps and in through the door.

I struggled up alone, with my lungs suddenly collapsed and yells from somewhere behind me in the darkness. I could hardly lift my feet, and yet I knew I must get up the steps and through that open door before somebody reached out from the black behind me and clutched me. It was a nightmare come to life. And then the footman caught my outstretched hand and dragged me in, the door slammed, and I sat down very quietly on the hall bench and fainted away.

(One of the people in this story insists that I was *not* left to drag myself up the steps alone, and that

he took me up and put me on the bench. But he
was excited, and I should know what really happened. He never even glanced at me.)

VII

I am sure, gentle reader—you can see what facil-
ity I am gaining; I would not have dared the
"gentle reader" in Chapter I—I am sure you will
think me stupid not to have understood the situation
by that time. But I did not. When I came to myself the footman was standing by, very stiffly, with
a glass of wine on a tray, and it was easy to see that
he knew I had lost my heel and that one of my lace
sleeves was gone. When I unclenched my hand and
found the necklace still there, and then dropped it
on the tray while I drank the wine, his jaw fell. But
where he had said, "Will you have some wine,
Miss?" before, now he said, "Shall I call 'Awkins,
my lady?"

"Don't call any one," I said wearily. "Or—I
wish you would find the—the person who just
came in with Sir George." And as he turned to go,
looking very puzzled, "Where am I?" I asked.

This really should have been said when I first
roused.

"At Wimberley Towers, my lady," the man answered, but he looked at me again curiously.

There was loud talking going on down the hall, and, as I sat, I could make out scraps of it. A man's voice, vaguely familiar, in an even monotone, followed by a shrill, excited one, also masculine.

"Berthold said there was a woman in the car, and that was what threw us off, sir. He's always seeing women."

A cold, high English voice came next and then another, but without the incisiveness of the earlier night—Sir George's voice, heavy and lifeless, yet with an undercurrent of scorn.

"Surely you do not think *that* necessary," he said.

The door was closed again, but a word reached me now and then, occasional raisins in the loaf of my darkness. (This is a better metaphor than I expected it to be, because I was loafing and the hall was dark!) There was talk about Three-Mile Lane, and somebody being accosted at a station, and a jingle of something that sounded like money, followed by the heavy tramping of men along a distant corridor and the closing of a door. Then a machine started somewhere outside with half a dozen shot-like reports followed by the soft hum of the engine. I had a queer feeling of being deserted in a strange place, and it came over me suddenly that I had heard there was a Lady Lethbridge at Wimberley, only they mostly called her Snooksie—English people use the queerest diminutives—and what if she came and asked me what I was doing and how I got there? Or perhaps Sir George would wire to town and bring down a lot of people to take me off to the Tower. The more I thought of it, the surer I felt that this was what was coming. I hoped they would let me change my gown, anyhow—white satin and what was left of bits of lace sleeves would look so queer being carried off to prison. And to think how I had dreamed of that gown, and how, because it was my first really dignified evening gown—all the rest being tulle and dancing frocks—how I had thought I would wear it just once and perhaps meet somebody who liked it terribly and me in it. And then I would lay it away, and some time later— much later—I would bring it out, a little yellow, and say, "Do you remember it?" And he would say, "Remember it? As long as I live." And I would say, "I thought of having baby's christening cloak made of it on account of the sentiment." And then he would hold out his arms and say, "Please don't!"

I had not heard any one come along the hall, because I was sniffling; so, when something touched me on the shoulder I looked up, and there *he* was, just as I had been—well, there he was. And he sat down on the bench beside me, in a puddle, and helped me find my handkerchief.

"I didn't mean to leave you," he said gently, "but

there was something that had to be attended to and couldn't wait. Can you walk as far as the library? There is a fire there and I will get you something dry. We can't go upstairs, because I suppose you don't care to let Blanche in on this?"

"Blanche?" I said, trying to balance on my one heel.

"My brother's wife," he explained. "Luckily, she's a little deaf, and Thad has gone up to see she doesn't snoop. What in the world is the matter? Just now you were quite tall and stately, and now you are hardly to my shoulder!"

So I told him about my heel, and he said he liked little women, and that no person who was just five feet two inches and had really curly hair was ever a Militant at heart, and that he had always thought young American girls were well heeled. It was an astonishing joke for an Englishman, until it developed that he had been living in California for a dozen years and was only home on a visit. And that his name was John, although he was mostly called Jack. When we were nicely settled by the library fire and the man had brought me a cup of tea that would have floated an egg, I asked him quite casually if there was a Mrs. John. He drew his chair up just opposite me and leaned forward with his chin in his hands.

"Not yet," he said.

Something made me draw my breath in sharply—
I think it was his tone—and I quite scalded my
throat with the tea. The fire was very hot, and little clouds of steam began to rise from my white satin.

"I have spoiled my gown," I said ruefully, "and
I had such plans for it."

"What kind of plans?" he asked, moving his chair
forward a little. "Do tell me. I'm always making
plans myself. And pretty soon, when you are dry
and the motor is ready, I shall have to take you
back to Ivry, and when we meet again—if we ever
do, for Daphne is going to kill me on sight—you will
be very, very formal and have both your heels."

"I hope you will forgive me," I said stiffly, "for
calling you a—a thief and locking you up and—
everything. I don't understand anything yet; it must
be because I am so sleepy."

"Poor little girl!" he said. "What you have gone
through! And as for forgiving you, you saved my
life tonight. Why, if you thought me a thief, did
you unload that revolver? If you tell me that I
will try to clear up the rest of the mysteries."

"I was afraid he might become excited and shoot
you," I returned simply. And he bent over and took
my hand.

"I hoped that was it," he said, just as simply. He
did not relinquish my hand.

(When I told Daphne the story I merely said of this: "I dried myself by the library fire.")

But suddenly I saw something that fairly made my blood chill in my veins. On the floor, at his very feet, the firelight dancing on their polished metal, lay a pair of handcuffs.

"Oh!" I cried and jumped to my feet, pointing. "You haven't been telling me the truth. They have given you a few minutes, and then they are coming back to take you away. Oh, don't let them to do it. I couldn't stand it!"

Yes, that is what I said. It was utterly shameless, of course, and no properly-behaved young woman would ever have said it. But no properly-behaved young woman would have kidnapped a Prime Minister, anyhow, and sat in a strange house while her hostess was asleep, drinking tea at four o'clock in the morning.

When I stood up *he* stood up, too, and looked down at me. "It is worth while having been a brute and a villain," he said soberly, "to hear that. I am not under arrest or going to be. The fact is that two entirely different and—if you will forgive me —nefarious schemes have been under way at the same time, and the lines crossed. You and I got tangled in them and nearly submerged. But that was not accident; it was destiny." He took my other hand.

At that absorbing moment the footman announced cautiously that the motor was at the door. It was horribly disappointing. From destiny to motor wraps is such a descent.

"Do we have to go right away?" I said.

VIII

It was just dawn when we started, one of the grey dawns that have a suggestion of pink, like a smoke-coloured chiffon over a rose foundation. The rain was over, and down in the valley below us lay shadowy white lakes of mist. I threw back my head and took a great breath.

"How beautiful!" I said. And he repeated, "Beautiful!" But he looked directly at me. I had a queer, thrilly feeling in the back of my neck.

And then we were flying down the hillside we had climbed so painfully the night before, and were dipping into the mist pools. Here and there grey shadows moved under the trees and resolved themselves first into rocks and then into sheep. (My descriptions are improving.) And as we went along he told me the story.

It seems he had come back from America for a visit, and on the second day of his stay the Wimberley Romney had been stolen by an expert picture thief posing as a tourist. He had caught a glimpse

of the visitor, so when the Romney was missed he
started out at once on the search, taking a motor
cycle. The whole countryside was roused, and three
detectives came down from London. But he had an
idea that he would find his man somewhere on the
moor, and he had lost himself there. After a night
under a rock he had found a cottage and got his
bearings. But the rain kept him there. He had
got as far as Harcourt Hall when another storm
came up. To his surprise he found the place almost
in decay, but the house open. He went in, dropped
asleep in the morning-room on a divan, wakened by
hearing me pass within a foot of where he lay, and
followed me. When I threw my necklace at him,
at first he was puzzled and amused. Later, he kept
it deliberately.

The next part of his story he had secured, I think
he said, by sitting on Bagsby's chest down the road,
after he had escaped by means of a broken shutter
from the rear room where we had locked him. Bagsby had had a puncture, and finding he had no time
to go back to Ivry for Daphne and the rest, he went
directly to the station. A train had just pulled out,
and a man in an ulster and travelling-cap was standing on the platform. He said, "The car for Gresham Place, sir"—which is what he was to say—
and the gentleman climbed in. But about two miles
out of town he (the passenger) had discovered he

had made a mistake, and demanded to be set down. But Bagsby had his orders. He carried him to the door of the Hall on the third speed, and the rest we knew.

"Then," I cried breathlessly, "Sir George was *not* —Sir George!"

"Far from it," he said cheerfully. "Poor old chap, what a front he put up! It seems that after he got the picture the alarm was raised too soon for him. He cut back over the country to make the railroad at Hepburn, and was overtaken by a storm. He found the Hall, crawled in through a rear window, concealed the picture there—it is still rolled in that carpet in the room where we hid, and waited for the storm to cease. But hunger drove him out. The picture off his hands, he made a break for it, got to Newbury just in time to miss the train, saw the constable and a posse approaching in a machine and bristling with guns, and at that minute Bagsby said: 'Gresham Place, sir.' From that time on he was virtually our prisoner, poor chap. He fell in with the plot because he didn't know what else to do. But what a shock it must have been when Bagsby dumped him back at the Hall, after he had walked six miles to get away from it."

"But you?" I exclaimed in bewilderment. "If you knew all the time——'

"I didn't. I did not recognise him until he took

off his mackintosh at the lodge. After that I had two problems: to capture him without alarming you, and to prevent the old-woman constable of the country from discovering us and dragging you and Daphne and all the rest into notoriety. Thanks to your coöperation it will never be known that a Suffragette plot to kidnap the Prime Minister was foiled last night."

"Then—the real Prime Minister"—I could hardly speak. I was horribly disappointed. I had hitched my wagon to a star and it had turned out to be a dirt-grubbing little meteorite.

"His grandchildren at Gresham Place took measles and they telegraphed him not to come."

There was silence for a moment. We were both thinking. Then:

"I am sure you managed it all very nicely," I conceded, "and I am very grateful now that you saved my necklace and—and all that. But if you think you captured *him* without alarming me you are mistaken. I shall never, never be the same person again. And as for the reward, I don't want it. I shall give it to Daphne for The Cause."

He looked around at me quickly. "To take my place," I amended. "I don't really care anything about voting, and, anyhow, I should never do it properly. They will welcome the money in my place, although doesn't it really belong to you?"

"I have already three rewards," he said, looking straight ahead. "The revolver which you emptied for fear our friend might shoot me, the limp little ball that is your handkerchief in my breast pocket, and this hour that belongs to me—the dawn, the empty world, and you sharing it all with me. Do you know," he went on, "that Daphne has seventeen pictures of you, and that I used to say I was going to marry you? There was one in very short skirts and long, white——"

"Mercy!" I broke in. "What is that over there?"

The mist had parted like a curtain, and on a lower road we saw, moving slowly, a strange procession. We stopped the machine and watched. Daphne was leading. She had the tail of her pink velvet gown thrown up over her shoulders and *she was in her stocking feet*. She carried her slippers dejectedly in her hand and she was ploughing along without ever troubling to seek a path. Behind her trailed the others. Most of them limped: all were mud-stained and dishevelled. An early sun-ray touched Violet and showed her wrapped, toga-fashion, in the hall banner. The red letters of "Votes for Women" ran around her diagonally like the stripes of a barber-pole. Poppy was trailing listlessly at the end of the procession, her gown abandoned to its fate and sweeping two yards behind her; a ribbon fillet with a blue satin rose that had nestled above her ear had become dislodged and the rose now hung dispiritedly at the back of her neck. Her short hair was all out of curl and lay matted in very straight little strands over her head.

And bringing up the tail of the procession—kicking viciously at Poppy's blue satin train in front of him—came Bagsby, a sheepish Bagsby loaded down with the hamper, a pail, a broom and a double-burner lamp with green shades. Even as he watched he took a hasty look ahead at the plodding back of his mistress, raised the lamp aloft and flung it against a stone. The crash was colossal, but not one head was turned to see the cause. They struggled along, sunk in deep bitterness and gloom.

And so they passed across our perspective, unseeing, unheeding, and the mists of the valley claimed them again.

The man beside me turned to me, his hands on the wheel. "Are you sorry you are not with them?" he asked gently. But I cowered back in my wraps and shook my head. "Take me home," I implored, "and please don't look at me again. If they all look like that I must be unspeakable!"

"We will get there ahead and wait for them together," he said. "And tonight I shall bring Thad and Blanche over to meet you. You—you won't mind seeing me again so soon?"

"Oh, no," I said hastily. "It—it is hours until evening."

"It will seem like eternities," he reflected.

"Yes, it will," I said.

(For it would to me, and if a man likes you and you like him, why not let him know it? And if he liked me the way I looked then, what would he think when he saw me clothed properly and in my right mind?)

He leaned over and kissed my hands as they lay in my lap. "Bless you!" he said. "I suppose you couldn't possibly wear that gown? Will you have to throw it away?"

"No," I announced, "I am going to lay it away. I—I may use it some time."

"How?" He was as curious as a child. "Are you going to make a banner of it, with gold fringe all round and 'Votes for Women' embroidered on it?"

"*No!*" I said decisively.

SAUCE FOR THE GANDER

SAUCE FOR THE GANDER

IT was on a Thursday evening that Basil Ward
came to Poppy's house at Lancaster Gate. We
had been very glum at dinner, with Poppy staring
through me with her fork half raised, and dabs of
powder around her eyes so I wouldn't know she had
been crying. Vivian's place was laid, but of course
he was not there. And after dinner we went up to
the drawing room, and Poppy worked at the kitchen
clock.

We heard Basil coming up the stairs, and Poppy
went quite pale. The alarm on the clock went off
just then, too, and for a minute we both thought
we'd been blown up.

Basil stood in the doorway—he's very good-looking, Basil, especially when he is excited. And he
was excited now. Poppy rose and stared at him. It
was very dramatic.

"Well?" she said.

"I'm deucedly sorry, Poppy," said Basil. "He
absolutely refuses. He says he'll stay. Says he
likes it. It's extremely quiet. He wants his pens
and some paper sent over—has an idea for the new
book."

Poppy's color came back in two spots in her cheeks.

"So he likes it!" she observed. "Very well. Then that's settled." She turned to me. "You've heard Basil, Madge, and you've heard me. That's all there is to it."

Poppy is very excitable, and as long as she had the clock in her hand Basil stayed near the door. Now, however, she put it down, and Basil came in.

"You and Vivian are a pair of young geese," he said to Poppy. "It's a horrible place."

"Vivian likes it."

"You are going to let him stay?"

"I didn't make the law. You men make these laws. Now try living up to them. When women have the vote——"

But Basil headed her off. He dropped his voice.

"That isn't the worst, Mrs. Viv," he said slowly. "He's—gone on a hunger strike!"

.   .   .   .

I'd been in England for six months visiting Daphne Delaney, who is my cousin. But visiting Daphne had been hard work. She is so earnest. One started out to go shopping with her, and ended up on a counter in Harrod's demanding of a mob of women hunting bargains in one-and-six kids (gloves) why they were sheep.

"Sheep!" she would say, eyeing them scornfully.

"Silly sheep who do nothing but bleat—with but one occupation, or reason for living, to cover your backs!"

Then two or three stately gentlemen in frock-coats would pull her down, and I would try to pretend I was not with her.

Now I believe in Suffrage. I own a house back home in America. Father gave it to me so I could dress myself out of the rent. (But between plumbers and taxes and a baby with a hammer, which ruined the paint, I never get much. Mother has to help.) The first thing I knew, the men voted to pave the street in front of the old thing, and I had to give up a rose-coloured charmeuse and pass over a check. But that isn't all. The minute the street was paved, some more men came along and raised my taxes because the street was improved! So I paid two hundred dollars to have my taxes raised! Just wait!

That made me strong for Suffrage. And of course there are a lot of other things. But I'm not militant. You know as well as I do that it's coming. The American men are just doing what father does at Christmas time. For about a month beforehand he talks about hard times, and not seeing his way clear and all that. And on Christmas morning he comes down stairs awfully glum, with one hand behind him. He looks perfectly miserable, but he's really having the time of his life. We always play up. We kiss him and tell him never to mind; maybe he can do it next year. And we're always awfully surprised when he brings his hand around with checks for everybody, bigger than they'd expected.

(That's the way with Suffrage in America. The men are holding off, and having a good time doing it. But they'll hand it over pretty soon, with bells on. The American man always gives his womenkind what they want, if they want it hard enough. Only he's holding off a little, so they'll appreciate it when they get it.)

It was after the affair of the Prime Minister that I left Daphne. We kidnapped him, you remember, only it turned out to be someone else, and Violet Harcourt-Standish got in awfully wrong and had to go to the Riviera. I really did not wish to kidnap him, but the thing came up at tea at Daphne's one day, and one hates to stay out of things.

Poppy was going on a motor trip just then, and when she asked me to go along, I agreed. I was spending a Sunday with her.

"I'm not running away, Madge," she explained. "But I'm stony broke, and that's the truth. I'll have to get back to work."

"You can't work in the motor."

Poppy paints, and makes a lot of money—mural decorations, you know, panels for public buildings, and all that sort of thing.

"I want sea, sea with mist over it, and rocks. And a cave——"

"Caves are damp. There are plenty of hotels."

"A cave," she said, examining her cigarette dreamily, "with the sea coming in against a setting sun, and the spray every color in the world. I think it's Tintagel, Madge."

Poppy is terribly pretty, and this is her story, not mine.

"That's a sweet frock," I said. "Did you hear that man to-day, when you were speaking at the Monument? He said, 'Bless its pretty 'eart——' "

Poppy's hair is the softest, straightest hair you ever saw, and her nose is short and childish. Her eyes are soft, too, and her profile is so helpless that the bobbies help her across the streets. But her full face is full of character.

"Was he in front of me?" she demanded.

"At the side."

We both understood. It was her profile again. She fell back in her chair and sighed.

"If you could address the House of Lords in profile," I said, "you'd get the vote."

"That's rot, you know," she retorted. But she coloured. She knew and she knew I knew that her new photographs were profile ones. And we both knew, too, that they were taken because Vivian Harcourt had demanded a picture.

"You're not doing the right thing, Poppy," I accused her. "For one day in the week that Viv sees you, there are six days for him to look at that picture."

"He isn't obliged to look at it at all."

"So long as women beg the question like that," I said severely, "just so long do they postpone serious consideration for the Cause."

She leaned back and laughed—rather rudely. The English can be very rude sometimes. They call it frankness.

"The ridiculous thing about you is that you don't know anything about the Cause," she said. "With you, it's a fad. It's the only thing you can't have, so you want it, little Madge. With some of us it's —well, I can't talk about it."

It made me furious. The idea of dedicating your life to a thing, and then being accused——

"I think enough of the Cause to stand out all day in a broiling sun," I snapped, "and be burnt to a cinder. Didn't I pass out your wretched literature for hours and make six shillings?"

"Don't call it wretched literature," she said gently. "But—now think a minute. If it came to a show-down—your own expression, isn't it—a question between one of these men who are so mad about you, Basil or any of the others—and the Cause, which would it be?"

"Both," I replied promptly.

She laughed again.

"You delightful little hypocrite!" she cried. "A Compromise, then! Not victory, but a truce! Oh, martyr to the Cause!"

"And you?"

"The Cause," she said, and turned, fullface to me.

Well, of course that was Poppy's affair. I believe in living up to one's conviction, and all that. But when you think of the lengths to which she carried her conviction, and the horrible situation that developed, it seems an exceedingly selfish theory of life. I believe in diplomatic compromise.

(I wrote the whole conversation that night to father, and he cabled a reply. He generally cables, being very busy. He said, "Life is a series of compromises. Who is Basil?")

Well, we got started at last. Poppy left in a raging temper over something or other—a bill before the house, I think. I was so busy getting packed that I forgot what it was, if I ever knew—and hardly spoke for twenty miles. But at Guildford she recovered her temper. It was the time of the Assizes, and the Sheriff was lunching at our hotel. His gilt coach was at the door, with a footman in wig and plush, white stockings and buckles, and a most magnificent coachman. Poppy's eyes narrowed. She pointed to the footman's ornamented legs.

"The great babies!" she said. "How a man loves to dress! Government, is it? Eighteenth century costumes and mediæval laws! Government—in gold lace and a cocked hat! Law in its majesty, Madge, with common sense and common justice in rags. *That* can vote, while you and I——" she stopped for breath.

The footman's calves twitched, but he looked straight ahead.

I got her into the building somehow or other. She looked quite calm, except that she was breathing hard. I confess that I thought she was ashamed of herself; I reminded her that she had promised to be quiet on this trip, and I told her, as firmly as I could, that it wasn't proper to make fun of a man's legs.

She powdered her nose and looked penitent and distractingly pretty.

"I'm sorry," she said. "It's this parade of authority that gets on my nerves, and this glittering show of half the people ruling all the people."

When she came back from ordering the luncheon she was smiling. I thought it was all over. (I am telling this incident, not because it belongs to the story, but because it sheds a light on Poppy's character, and perhaps explains what came later.)

"Luncheon!" she said, cheerfully, "with strawberries as big as a teacup, and clotted cream."

I think my mind was on the clotted cream, for I

followed her past one dining-room to a second, a long, low room, full of men. She pushed me in ahead.

"I—I think it's the wrong room, Poppy," I said. "There's the———"

It *was* the wrong room, and she knew it. The Sheriff was at the centre table and near him was a great serving stand, with hot and cold roasts and joints.

I tried to back out, but at that moment Poppy slammed the door and locked it.

"Don't yell!" she said to me under her breath, and *dropped something ice-cold down my back. The key!*

About half the men started to their feet. Poppy raised a hand.

"Gentlemen," she said, "you need not rise! I have a few things I would like to say while you finish luncheon. I shall be entirely orderly. The question of the Suffrage———"

They dodged as if she had been loaded with shrapnel instead of a speech. They shouted and clamored. They ordered us out. And all the time the door was locked and the key was down my back.

"Poppy!" I said, clutching her arm. "Poppy, for the love of heaven———"

She had forgotten me absolutely. When she finally turned her eyes on me, she never even saw me.

"The door is locked, gentlemen," she said. "Locked and the key hidden. If you will give me five minutes——"

But they would not listen. The Sheriff sat still and ate his luncheon. Time might come and time might go, tides flow and ebb, old eras give way to new—but the British lion must be fed. But once I caught his eye, and I almost thought it twinkled. Perish the thought! The old order wink at the new!

They demanded the key. The lunch hour was over. The Assizes waited. In vain Poppy plead for five minutes to talk.

"After that, I'll turn over the key," she promised.

The only way she could have turned over the key was, of course, to take me into a corner, stand me on my head and jounce it out! I was very nervous, I'll confess. No one had laid a hand on ⸢oppy as yet. She was so young and good looking, and the minute anybody loomed very close, she turned her baby profile to him and he looked as if he'd been caught gunning for butterflies.

Finally, however, the noise becoming a tumult, and Poppy and I forced back against the door, the Lord High Sheriff—which sounds like Gilbert & Sullivan—approached. The crowd made respectful way for him.

"Now, young ladies," he said, "this has been an

agreeable break in our long day. But—all pleasant things must end. Open the door, please."

"Will you give me five minutes?" Poppy demanded. "I'm a tax-payer. I help to pay the people in this room. I have a right to be heard."

"Open the door," said the Sheriff.

"No."

"Then give up the key, and one of my men——"

I caught his arm. I couldn't stand it another minute. It is all well enough for Poppy to say it was cowardly, and that the situation was ours until I gave it away. The key was not down *her* back.

"Break the lock," I said frantically. "The—the key is where I can't get it."

He was really twinkling now, but the crowd around was outraged for him and his dignity.

"You didn't swallow it, did you?" he asked in an undertone.

"It's down the back of my frock," I replied.

Poppy said afterwards that I cried and made a scene and disgraced her generally. It is not true. If tears came, they were tears of rage. It is not true that I cried on the Sheriff's breast. I only leaned my head against his arm for a minute, and he was not angry, for he patted my shoulder. I am terribly fond of Poppy, but she is not always reasonable, as you will see.

There had been a great deal of noise. I remember

hearing echoes of the dining-room excitement from the hallway beyond the door, and some one pounding. They were breaking the lock from the outside. All the time Poppy was talking in her lovely soft voice. She said:

"Since woman is called on to obey the laws, she ought to have a voice in making them——"

"Hear, hear!" cried somebody.

"Since she doesn't make them, why should she obey them?" demanded Poppy, lifting violet eyes to the crowd.

"I didn't make the Ten Commandments," said a voice from the rear of the room, "but I'll get hell just the same if I break them. What have you got to say about that?"

Poppy was stumped for once. I believe it was the most humiliating moment of her public life.

Luckily the lock broke just then, and we were hustled out of the room. There was a crowd in the hall, and it was most disagreeable. I expected to be arrested, of course—although I'd been arrested before, and if one is sensible and eats, it is not so bad —but the crowd, feeling it had the best of things with the Ten Commandments, was in high good humor. They let us by without a word and the Sheriff himself stood on the steps while we got into our car.

Just as Poppy's chauffeur got the engine started,

the landlord ran out and demanded the key. Poppy told the chauffeur to go on, in a frantic voice, but he hesitated. All the majesty of British law was there on the steps, and the gold coach was waiting. Of course, to be arrested for disturbing the peace with a suffrage speech is one thing, but theft is another. I threw a pleading glance at the Sheriff, and he came slowly down the steps. Men with wands kept the crowd back. The fat coachman with the wig did not turn his head, but the footman at the coach door leered and avenged his calves. Even Poppy went a little pale.

"Quick," said the Sheriff, ferociously, in a low tone, "give me something that looks like a key, and then get away as quickly as you can."

I opened my pocketbook. The only thing that was even the size of a key was my smelling salts bottle. So I gave him that, and he covered it with his big hand. Then, still frowning savagely, he made us a lordly gesture to move on.

(Have you ever been in the Forum Club building that Poppy decorated? The staircase walls are wonderful—crowds of women, poor and old, young and rich with clouds around them and so on, all ascending toward a saintly person with a key—Saint Peter, or somebody. Well, the saint is the Sheriff at Guildford, and the key is a salts bottle, if you look closely.)

We slept at Bournemouth that night. Or rather, we didn't sleep. Poppy sat up half the night trying to think of an answer to the ten commandment thing. She said she'd get that again—she felt it—and what was she to say? I had recovered the key and my good humor by that time, but I could not help much. Seeing her so disturbed, I had not the heart to tell her what I suspected. But I was sure that I had seen Vivian Harcourt on the edge of the crowd at Guildford. It would have made her furious to think that she was under any sort of espionage. But Vivian was following us, I felt confident, with enough money to bail us out if she did anything reckless. He knew her, you see.

That is why all the rest of it seems so silly. Vivian knew Poppy; he knew her convictions, and her courage. For him to do the baby thing later was stupid. And anyhow, if it was hard on him, what was it for me?

Poppy slept late in the morning, and I got up and went down to the pier, a melancholy place, wet with morning mist and almost deserted. There were rows of beach chairs, and bathing machines and over-turned boats littering the beach, and not a soul in sight but a few fishermen. I sat there and thought of Newport on a bright July morning, with children and nurses on the sand, and throngs of people, and white sailboats and nice young men in flannels

—— I was awfully homesick for a minute. And it came over me, too, that I had no particular business helping the Cause in England, and having keys put down my back, and giving up my gold-topped salts bottle, which was a present from Basil Ward, when all the time the Cause at home was fighting just as grimly and much more politely.

Vivian was on the pier, at the very end. He was sitting looking out, with his finger hooked around his cigarette (which is Cambridge fashion, I believe, or may be the King does it) and looking very glum.

"Where is she? In jail?" he demanded.

"She's asleep, poor thing," I said.

He snorted.

"Lots of sleep I've had," he said. "Look here, Madge, is she going to take her vacation by locking up Sheriffs all along the route? Because if she is, I'm going back to London."

"I think it very likely," I replied, coldly. "You'd better go back anyhow; she'll be murderous if she knows she's followed."

He groaned.

"I can't leave her alone, can I?"

"I'm along."

He laughed. It was rude of him.

"You!" he said. "Madge, tell me honestly— *where* was the key?"

"She put it down my back."

He fairly howled with joy. I hated him. But he calmed before long, and offered me a cigarette as a peace offering. I declined.

"You'd better go along," he said. "She may need the—back again. Madge, is there any chance for me with her?"

"Well, she likes you, when you are not in the way."

"I'd be in the way now, I suppose, if I turned up to-night at—where do you stop?"

"At Torquay. Look here, Vivian, I've just thought of something. She's put out about a thing a man said yesterday. She wants an answer. She's got arguments, but what she wants is a retort—about six words and smart. If you could give her one, she'd probably forgive you hanging around, and all that."

So I told him about the ten commandments and Poppy knowing she'd get it again and sitting up to worry it out. He said it was easy. He'd have something to break his appearance at Torquay. But it wasn't as easy as it seemed at first. I left him sitting there, looking out to sea, with a notebook on his knee. He called after me that he'd follow us, a few miles behind, but he wouldn't turn up until he had thought of something worth while.

According to Basil, it was he who finally thought

of something. It seems that Vivian wrote out pages
of a reply, saying that if the questioner compared
man-made law with the ten commandments, then he
made Parliament and the House of Lords divine,
and that this was a *reductio ad absurdum*, which is
Greek or something for ridiculous. But he almost
went mad trying to make it short, and it wasn't
funny at all. Whereas, as he knew very well, the
only chance the speaker had, in such a case, was to
get a laugh. What he really needed was a retort,
not a reply.

We made rather slow progress. In the first place,
Poppy learned that the *chauffeur*, who was a new
one and quite intelligent, was not in favour of suffrage, and for hours we crawled along, while she argued with him. And in the second place, we stopped
frequently to nail up posters along the roadside.
Vivian said later that he trailed us quite easily, and
that there were times when he was only one curve
in the road behind. He used to get out and putter
over the engine to pass the time and let us get ahead.
He did not appear at Torquay, so I knew he wasn't
getting along well with the ten commandments.

But except being put out of a hotel at Exeter for
discovering a member of Parliament there, in bed
with the gout, and flinging some handbills in through
the transom, the rest of the trip was very peace-
ful. Dartmoor put Poppy into a trance; the heather

was in bloom, and she made sketches and colour bits, and lay back in the car in a sort of dream, planning the next winter's work.

She was irritable when she was disturbed, too. The creative instinct is a queer thing. Once Bootles, the chauffeur, asked her a question when she was trying to catch some combination or other, and she answered him sharply.

"When the women go to vote, Miss," he said, turning around and touching his cap, "who is going to mind the children?"

"We intend to establish a messenger service," said Poppy, with a crayon in her mouth.

"A *messenger* service?" Bootles' eyes stuck out.

"Yes. To summon the fathers home from the pubs to hold the babies."

(A "pub" of course is an English saloon.)

The T. C. matter was still bothering Poppy at intervals. She knew as well as anyone that she needed a laugh in her retort, and as you have seen, Poppy is too earnest to be funny. I said this to Basil Ward the night we got to Tintagel

Poppy was tired, and went to bed early. I walked out on the terrace, and Basil was there. He said Viv had sent for him on the T. C. matter, and he had something in view.

"He gave it up, poor chap," he said. "He isn't humorous, you know. As a matter of fact, he and

Poppy are both so bally serious that it makes me wonder how they'll hit it off."

"If she's as earnest about matrimony as she is about Suffrage," I said, "she'll be a sincere wife."

Basil said nothing. We had walked out to the edge of the cliff, and were leaning against the rough stone parapet.

"It's rather nice, isn't it," he said suddenly. "Here we are, almost at Land's End, and the old Atlantic —Madge, will you give me a perfectly honest answer to a question?"

I braced myself.

"Yes."

"Did you stay over here in England because your whole heart is in the Cause?"

"Ye—es."

"Your *whole* heart?"

"Our motives are always mixed, Basil," I said kindly. "It would have been awfully silly to have endured that miserable spring and not have stayed for June and July."

"You get a great many cablegrams from America."

"That," I said, with dignity, "is of course my own affair."

"About the Cause?"

"Not—always."

"From a man, of course."

"Yes," I said sweetly, and went back to the hotel.

I broke the news to Poppy about Vivian and she stormed. But suddenly she stopped, with a calculating gleam in her eye.

"He's a fool to follow me," she said, "but he has gleams of intelligence, Madge. I shall put the T. C. matter up to him!"

So I sent Viv a note that night. You see one must manage Poppy

"Dear Viv: She knows and the worst is over. Breakfast early and keep out of the way until noon. She is going to work, and anyhow, it will make her curious. If you have a good retort to the T. C. business, don't give it at once. It would humiliate her. Then, when you've given it to her, if she's pleased, you can ask her *the other*. She's silly about you, Viv, but she won't acknowledge it to herself.

Madge.

P. S. Don't make any stipulation about Suffrage, but make her promise to let you do and think as you like. *Be sure*. Get her to write it, if you can. I happen to know that if she marries you, she hopes you'll take alternate Sundays with her at the Monument, so she can speak at Camberwell.

M."

Poppy came down to breakfast in her best morning frock, looking lovely, and sat with her profile to the room. I thought she watched the door, too, and she took only an egg, although she usually has a kipper also.

But neither of the men showed up. She loitered over the *Times*, but at last she got her sketching things, and we went out to the cliff head, where there's a bench. It is a long tongue of rock, about twenty feet wide or so, and far below, on each side, the ocean. There was a rough-haired pony out there also, and the three of us were crowded. The pony wanted sugar or something, and kept getting in the way. Poppy sketched, but her heart wasn't in it and at every new halloo from some tourist exploring King Arthur's ruins (The Castle, of course) she looked up expectantly.

At last I caught sight of Basil waving to me from the hotel, and I went back. I left Poppy there alone, pretending to sketch, although it was perfectly clear to every one that the only view she had was of the pony's mangy side. Shortly after, I saw Vivian, in walking tweeds, going along one of the sheep's paths toward her, and looking very handsome and determined.

Basil and I sat on the terrace and "concentrated." It was my idea.

"Will her to take him," I said.

"I am," said Basil, looking at me.

"She's so pretty," said I.

"Lovely!" said Basil.

"And it's such a *natural* thing," I went on. "He has a lot of character, and he's gentle as well as firm."

"I thank you," said Basil, and bowed.

"I don't believe," I said severely, "that you are concentrating."

The pony had got around behind the bench, and we lost them for a moment. But the little beast moved off just then, and it was like lifting a curtain. Poppy's head was on Vivian's shoulder.

"Good old Viv!" said Basil. "Happy chap!" and sighed.

.   .   .   .   .   .

I met Vivian as I went down to luncheon. He was coming up three stairs at a time, but he stopped and drew me into a corner.

"All fixed," he said. "You're a trump, Madge. The T. C. did it. She's promised all sorts of things."

"And you?" I demanded. I thought he evaded my eye.

"I?" he said. "Well, I've agreed not to interfere with her career. That's only reasonable."

"And—Suffrage?"

"She's going to be less militant," he said. "Of course, her conviction is the same. I want her to stand by her principle. I wouldn't respect her if she didn't."

It didn't quite satisfy me. I knew Poppy. **But**

he was so happy that I said nothing. After all, what could I say? Viv after all had never opposed Suffrage, except in its militant form—although I don't believe he had felt the necessity for it. But the trouble was that Poppy was a born militant, a born aggressor. And he had promised her the strength of her convictions!

(I wrote it all to father that afternoon and his cablegram came when I was back in London again and settled.

"No great revolution ever accomplished without bloodshed.")

PART SECOND

WHEN Poppy and Vivian had been married and gone to Brittany, I went back to Daphne's. Daphne was very discouraging about them. I remember her standing by the fire and orating, with her tea cup in her hand.

"There's a loss somewhere—bound to be," she said. Daphne is short and stout, and wears her hair short and curled over her head with an iron. "Either Suffrage loses her, or she loses a husband. I've watched it. It doesn't do, Maggie," which is her pet name for me. "A Suffragist as valuable as Poppy should not marry. You remember what Jane Willoughby's husband said to her, that he expected The Cause for his wife to be himself, and that if she'd rather raise votes for women than a family of children she would have to choose at once. When she asked him why she couldn't do both, he went to Africa!"

"Without giving her an answer?"

"Bless the child, there isn't any answer! It isn't wisdom that takes refuge in silence. It's silly, besotted, dumbheaded idiocy."

"Viv isn't an imbecile," I said feebly.

"He's a male," she snapped, and ran her fingers up through her fringe, so that she appeared to stand in a gale of wind.

The first blow fell about a week after. Poppy and Vivian came home from their wedding trip. They were settled in Viv's house in Lancaster Gate, and one part of the wings was being turned into a studio for Poppy, with a glass roof. Vivian is the playwright, you know, and his study was to be beneath her work shop, with a private staircase connecting. She was most awfully happy. She'd brought home some stunning sketches, and her first work was going to be his study walls.

Basil and I were asked to dinner. Poppy wanted to talk over her plans with us, and there was no one else. Poppy was radiant. We drank to the pony at Tintagel, and to the key at Guildford, and to the new play and the new paintings. The thing was a great success until half way through the dinner, when suddenly Poppy said:

"By the way, Viv, the income tax man was here today."

I felt, for some reason, as I had felt when the key went down my back.

Viv smiled, and went to his doom.

"Just imagine, Basil," he said. "The sweet young person across the table made more than I did last year! Four thousand pounds!"

"I'm too commercially successful to think I have any real genius," said Poppy, complacently.

"And some small sum the same sweet young person will have to pay over to the tax man," Basil observed.

Poppy raised her violet eyes.

"I don't intend to pay it," she said.

Vivian put down his glass.

"That's what Madge would call a 'bluff,'" he said, with his eyes on her. "You'll be obliged to pay it, dearest. You know that."

"'Taxation without representation' is what it amounts to." Poppy's face was dangerously agreeable. "The American colonies seceded, didn't they, for something like that? I paid it last year, but I made up my mind then I'd never do it again."

Basil was looking very uncomfortable.

"I gave you the privilege of your convictions," said Viv, stiffly. "Of course, if that's your intention, there is nothing more to be said."

Poppy looked puzzled.

"But it *is* wrong, isn't it?" she demanded. "Surely that's the a.b.c. of the reason for the discontent of Englishwomen."

"The principle may not be entirely equitable. Few laws work equally well for all." Vivian now, a little white about the lips. "But, such as it is, it's the law of your country."

"I didn't choose my country, or make it's laws," Poppy said coldly. "I have a right to protest; I'll not pay it."

Now, as I have said before, motives are seldom unmixed. I think what Poppy meant to do was simply to register a protest, refuse to pay, make a lot of fuss about it. If they sent her to jail, being the prominent person she was—she was the Honourable Poppy, I think I forgot to say that before—it would make a lot of feeling. She did not mind jail very much. She'd been there twice. Then, having asserted her principles, she could get sick or go on a hunger strike, and Vivian would pay the tax and get her out.

Basil laughed with assumed cheerfulness.

"Then Viv is stuck for the tax," he said.

Vivian looked across the table and met Poppy's eyes.

"That's hardly what you are getting at, is it?" he asked. "Your protest is against the imposition of the tax, isn't it? It's a matter of principle, isn't it? My paying it wouldn't help."

"I have not asked you to pay it."

"As a matter of fact, I haven't the slightest intention of paying it, Poppy. You put me in an absurd position, that's all."

We had finished dinner, and the men went up to

the drawing room with us. A funny thought struck Basil on the way up. He chuckled.

"Of course, Viv," he said, "if Poppy sticks to that, you'll have to do something. There's the Husband's Liability Act. You're liable, you know."

Basil is a barrister.

Well, we talked of other things and pretended not to notice Vivian's strained eyes and Poppy's high color. She took me off after a time to see the new studio, and it did not take me long to tell her what I thought.

"It's absurd," I said. "Do you expect to break down iron bars by banging a head against them?"

"It's my head," she said sulkily.

"Not at all. It's Vivian's. They will jail him."

"I didn't make the law."

"Like the man with the Ten Commandments at Guildford!" I retorted. "He didn't make them, but you know where he said he'd go if he broke them. By the way, Poppy, I've always meant to ask you, did you ever get a retort ready in case the T. C. came up again?"

But the men came in just then, and I did not learn. It was rather a ghastly evening. We were all most polite and formal and Basil took me home. I told him about my house at home in the United States, and the way I'd been treated, and having nothing at the end of a year but plumber's bills and tax receipts.

"I'm glad you haven't any particular income," he said at last. "That's one element of discord removed."

"I don't understand."

"Yes, you do," he said calmly. "You know exactly what I mean, and what I hope and what I feel. I don't dare to say it, because if I start I'll—Madge, I shall *not* propose to you until my Uncle Egbert dies. I don't want you until I can support you comfortably—that's a lie. I want you damnably, all the time."

I do not remember that we said anything more until we reached Daphne's. Then, as he helped me out, I said:

"How old is Uncle Egbert?"

"Eighty-six," he replied grimly, and went away without shaking hands.

Well, to go back to Poppy, for of course it is her story I am telling, not mine. Mother came over soon after that and I went with her to Mentone for two months. Then she went back to America from Genoa, and I went back to London. Mother is the sweetest person in the world, and I adore her, but she represents the old-fashioned woman, and of course I stand for the advanced. For instance, she was much more interested in Basil Ward than in the

Cause, and she absolutely disapproved of Poppy's stand about the income tax.

"I don't care to discuss the Cause," she said to me. "We have trouble enough now with only the men voting. Why should we double our anxieties?"

"That's silly, mother," I retorted. "Because one baby is a trouble and naughty sometimes, should one have only one child?"

Basil met me at Charing Cross, and I knew there was something up by the very way his stick hung to his arm.

"How's everything?" I asked, when he had called a cab and settled me in it. "How nice and sooty it is, after the Riviera!"

"Filthy hole!" said Basil grumpily. "Haven't had a decent day since you left."

(This was remarkable, because the papers had all said the weather in London was wonderful for that time of year.)

"And Poppy?"

"Poppy's a fool," Basil broke out. "I'm glad you're back, Madge. Maybe you can do something with her."

But he refused to tell me anything further. He asked if I would mind going directly to Lancaster Gate, and sat back in a corner eyeing me most of the way.

"You make me nervous," I said at last. "If you can't look at me pleasantly, why look at all?"

"I can't help looking at you, and I'm blessed if I can look pleasant. Madge, just how much is your heart and soul in the—er—Cause?"

Well, I was pretty tired of being questioned all the time. I said:

"There isn't any sacrifice I wouldn't make for it."

"If you were married——"

"I wouldn't marry a man who didn't think as I do."

He seemed to drop back further into his corner. The whole thing puzzled me. For Basil said nothing, but looked dejected and *beaten*, somehow. And yet he had always believed that women should vote.

We found Poppy in her studio, but Viv's workroom below was empty and the door into the passage stood open. His desk was orderly and his pens in a row. It looked queer. Poppy was painting, standing before a huge canvas and looking very smeary; she gave me a cheek to kiss, and she was thin! Positively thin!

"You're looking very fit, Maggie," she said, without a smile. "We've missed her, haven't we, Basil?"

Basil grunted something. Suddenly it occurred to me that he and Poppy hardly glanced at one another, and that he was still holding his hat and gloves. Their constraint, and Viv not around and everything—I was very uncomfortable. Of course, if Basil cared for Poppy and I used to think he did, and if Vivian had found it out—

"No, thanks, Poppy," said Basil, "I'll—I'll drop in again."

"Crumpets for tea!" said Poppy. They'd engaged the cook for her crumpets.

"Thanks awfully," Basil muttered and having said something about seeing me again very soon, he got out. I stared after him. Could this be Basil the arrogant? Basil the abject? This brooding individual who did nothing but stare at me as if he were trying to work something out!

Poppy came over to me, with her fists in the pockets of her painting apron, and looked down at me.

"Frightened, like all the rest!" she said. "They say I'm responsible for hundreds of broken engagements! They made the law themselves, and now, when they see it in operation, they squeal."

It came over me then; Poppy's strained eyes, and her painting without a cigarette, and Basil looking so queer.

"Then Viv——"

"Viv is in jail, my dear," she said. "Men made the law, of course, but I wish you'd hear them! The Husband's Liability Act, child. A married woman's husband is responsible for her debts. I refused to pay my income tax as taxation without representation. Viv got stubborn, and said *he* wouldn't. Result, the entire male population screaming for help, engaged men breaking with Suffragist fiancées, the population prospects of the country poor, and—Viv in jail!"

I could hardly speak for a minute.

"That—that's what is wrong with Basil?"

"Of course I'm sorry, Maggie. You see, you have an income of your own and at any moment, by refusing to pay the tax on it, you can send Basil to jail."

"If he were any sort of a husband," I said furiously, "he could pay the tax and save all the trouble."

"Not at all. The men have banded together. They call it the Husband's Defence! They take turns at visiting Viv, and sending him books and things. It's—it's maddening."

Poppy asked me to stay with her. She was really in a bad way. She wasn't eating or sleeping, and that very night a crowd of men gathered in front of the house, and hissed and called her things. One of them made a speech. We listened from behind the curtains. He said his wife was holding out her taxes on him and he expected to "go up" the next day. Poppy went out on the balcony and tried to tell them why she had done it, and that it was a matter of principle, and all that. But they would not listen, and only jeered. She came back into the drawing room quite beaten, and covered her face with her hands.

It was the next evening that Basil told us that Vivian, feeling as he did that he represented the married men of the Kingdom and that he stood for principle also, had gone on a hunger strike!

. . . .

After all, it was Daphne, who came to the rescue. She came over to luncheon the day after and found Poppy in bed with cold cloths on her head, and her wedding ring off. Daphne sniffed.

"You and Viv are two children," she said. "You're a silly for thinking you can beat the government at its own game, which is taxation, and Viv's a fool for letting you be one."

Poppy is not placid of disposition, and she flung the cold cloths at Daphne and ordered her out. But Daphne only wrung out the cloths and hung them up, and raised the shades.

"You haven't got a headache; you have a pain in your disposition," she said. "Put this on again."

And Poppy put on her wedding ring.

"Now," said Daphne. "You won't pay this money as a matter of principle, and Viv won't, for the same reason. I won't because I haven't got it:

Madge probably ditto. But it must be paid. Have you got it in the house?"

Poppy nodded.

"In notes?"

"Yes."

"Where?"

"In my jewel case."

"Very well. Now," said Daphne, "Madge and I are going to fix this thing up. You are not to know anything about it. You can swear to that later on, if the question comes up. Is there any place in your studio where you keep money?"

"In the table drawer."

"Very well. Tonight before you go to bed put that money there. Early tomorrow morning send a maid to the drawer. If, by any chance, it is not there, send for the police."

Poppy was sitting up in bed, her eyes narrowed.

"The door of that wing is always locked. Viv has one key; I have the other."

"Never mind about the keys," said Daphne, loftily. "Now lie back and take a nap. Madge and I are going to look at the new picture. And I'm taking Madge home to dinner. I want her to go with me to the Edgware Road meeting tonight."

We did not look at the picture very long. Daphne's lips were shut tight, and I was feeling very queer. I knew what Daphne meant to do—to have the exact amount of Poppy's tax stolen from the table, and reported to the police. And later on in the day to have it sent to the tax office in Poppy's name. Poppy could swear she had not done it and point to the robbery. But by that time it would be credited to her name, and Viv would be free.

"It's a knot," said Daphne, running her fingers through her hair. "It's past un-tying. We have to cut it."

I know it sounds silly now and father has advised me never to tell mother, but it seemed the only thing at the time. Here were Viv and Poppy at an *impasse*, as one may say, and things getting worse every day— Viv on a hunger strike, and Poppy's work waiting, and the vote, which was our natural solution, as far off as ever.

"I'll unlock a window in Viv's study," said Daphne, "and you can come back after midnight and crawl in. I'd do it, but I'm too fat. Once in, you've only to go up the little staircase to the studio, and get the money. The key's always in the side door. You can let yourself out."

"But I don't like it, Daphne."

"A broken window," said Daphne, "would look a lot better. More natural, you know. Here, hold a pillow."

She raised one of Viv's windows a little—we were in his study—and she put her arm outside, with a paper weight in her hand. A smart tap, and a pane fell in on my pillow. We listened but no servants had come running and the house next door was closed and shuttered.

Daphne is very clever. She unlocked the window, drew the shade as it had been before, and put the glass in a little heap on the floor. The area was outside, about five feet below.

"I could never do it," I protested. "I—I haven't your courage, Daffie. Be a dear and do it yourself."

"Have to be at Edgware Road," said Daphne. "After all, Poppy's your friend. You made the match, didn't you?"

"But if I'm arrested——"

"You won't be. Jane Willoughby is going with me tonight. I'll lend her some of your clothes and a veil. She can make a speech in your name. There's an alibi for you!"

Now it sounded all right at the time, but looking back, it seems queer. For of what use is an alibi if the police have you? But one thing I would not do. I would not climb in the window. Daphne finally put me behind one of Poppy's canvases in the studio on a chair.

"They'll *think* you broke in, which answers as well," she said. "And you can get the money and let yourself out the side door without any trouble."

"I sha'n't have any dinner," I reminded her. But

she said she'd have something ready for me at home after I'd committed my crime, and went down the staircase whistling.

I shall never forget that awful night. I was most uncomfortable. There was a chance that the servants, locking up, would go into Viv's study and find the glass, although it was behind the curtain. But I'd seen Peters lock up before. He stood in a doorway and looked at each window, and if the curtains did not blow the house was safe. Luckily there was no wind that evening!

But I hated the whole thing. It got darker and darker and things scrambled in the walls. Poppy brought the money and put it in a drawer but of course I did not speak to her. She had to be able to swear she knew nothing. She kissed Viv's picture which she had painted, and trotted out again, sighing. Peters did not discover the broken window in the den below, because he never even went to look. And I felt very dreary, with no one really caring for me, and so far from America, and men—like Basil, for instance—acting so strange and uneasy.

Of course I could have taken the money and gone, as soon as it was dark. But a policeman took up a position outside the area door, and waited for somebody. He and Peters had a few words about Poppy's maid, and the policeman said he would see her if he had to stay there all night. He stayed for hours.

I got the money and put it in my handbag, and because I did not wish to get it mixed with my own, I put it by itself in one of the pockets. Then I think I dozed for two or three hours, for when waking the street was quiet and the policeman had gone away. I was stiff, tired, and out of humor, and I started down the little staircase past Viv's study to the area door. As I reached the bottom, somebody tried the lock outside. I nearly fainted. I turned and ran up in the dark, and the door below opened. A man came in stealthily and went directly to Vivian's den. And just then a church clock struck two.

I was frightened. It seemed to me that as soon as he ransacked the room below, he'd come up to the studio. Perhaps he knew about the money. Burglars seem to be able to *smell* money. And the idea of being caught in the studio, as in a *cul de sac*, made me panicky. I clutched my bag, and slipped down the staircase, past Vivian's door. The burglar was there, going through Viv's desk, with a light turned on and a cap down over his eyes.

I forgot to be cautious then. I bolted for the door, flung it open—it was a patent lock, with a knob inside—and stepped out into the night air and the policeman's arms.

"Easy a bit, hold girl!" he said. "Hi'm 'ere and you're 'ere. What's the 'urry?" He held me off

and looked at me. Luckily I'd never seen him before. "Quick with your 'ands, ain't you! In you
goes and in five minutes out you pops!"

"If you think I'm a burglar," I said haughtily,
"I'm nothing of the sort. I'm——" It came over
me, all at once, that I'd better not say I was a friend
of Poppy's. You see she was being watched very
closely. If I was searched, and the exact amount
of her income tax in my pocket, it would look very
queer, and the whole thing would be out, of course.
"The burglar you followed is still in the house," I
said. "He's in Mr.—in the study, just beyond
that door."

"None of that, young woman," he said, sternly.
"You'll just come along with me! 'Ouse-breaking
it is; I watched you in and I watched you hout."

He took me by the arm, and I went along. There
was nothing else to do. I tried to drop my hand
bag as we went, but he heard it and picked it up. I
was rather dazed. The only thing I could think of
was that for the sake of the Cause and Poppy I must
not tell who I was. But I begged him to send
an officer to Poppy's house, because there *was* a burglar in it, probably after the idea of Vivian's new
novel.

At the police station they telephoned Poppy, and
here she made her terrible mistake. She said afterwards that if Daphne had only explained she'd have

known. But she thought it was all a part of the plot, and she went back to her studio and said she'd lost the money out of a table drawer. She told how it was, in notes and gold, and, of course, they found the exact amount in my bag. She says that when they told her they had it and a young woman too, she almost swooned. She tried to find Basil, but he was not in his rooms and Daphne had been arrested at Edgware Road and was *incommunicado!*

Poppy's position was pitiable. She didn't know what to do. If she declared the plot and freed me, all London would laugh, and the Cause would suffer. If she did not declare the plot, I would get a prison sentence. I have drawn a poor picture of Poppy if you think I stood a chance against The Cause.

That is how things stood the next morning; Daphne, Vivian and I in jail, and Poppy in hysterics. Then a curious thing happened. The evening papers announced that Vivian had paid the tax for Poppy and was free. Viv repudiated the payment—said he had not done it, and refused his liberty.

"Mr. Harcourt," said one paper, "is quite thin and shows the strain of his confinement. He is apparently cheerful, but very feeble, supporting himself by the back of a chair while he stood. His eyes flashed, however, as he stated that the Income Tax office could not legally accept the payment, as it was not his money. If any of his supporters had, in mistaken zeal, taken a collection for this purpose, he could only regret their action and refuse to profit by it."

At this time I had refused to talk and Poppy was in bed.

But on the next day the *Times* published a letter, signed "Only a Man" which stirred the whole thing up again. The writer declared that the tax had been paid with Vivian's own money, that the writer himself had stolen it out of a desk in Mr. Harcourt's house, that it had been sent by messenger to the proper authorities, and a receipt issued, which was appended. And that, in other words, while Mr. Harcourt was to be lauded for his principles, his refusal to accept his liberty was now absurd. Also, the writer was under the impression that an innocent person was being held for his crime.

This story being investigated by the authorities and Poppy's recovering enough to come down and identify me, furiously indignant at my detention and outraged that I had not told my name and how I came to be leaving her house at that hour, which she said was because we had had a long talk about the next campaign, I was freed at last. It leaked out like this:

(a) Viv was free with no loss of principle.

(b)   Poppy's tax was paid, with no loss of principle.

(c)   "A Mere Man" was not apprehended.

(d)   Basil reappeared, after a heavy cold.

I was not present when Viv and Poppy met, owing to some formalities of my release. I drove to the house with Poppy's money in my bag, and went up unannounced. Viv was not pale and wan. He looked rested and fit, and Poppy was on his knee. When I went in she moved to the arm of his chair, but no further, and she kept her profile toward him.

They were very apologetic and said how sorry they were, and Poppy said she knew Daphne and I meant well, but that one wrong would never help another. I was speechless with rage, and I took from my bag her money and held it out to her.

"Of course," I said, "Vivian has no idea of who 'A Mere Man' is?"

"None whatever," said Viv shamelessly.

"That's curious," I observed. "I saw him quite distinctly, you know, as I went down the stairs."

(I had—his back!)

I went out, with my head up. They called to me, and I think Vivian started to follow. But I got into a taxicab and drove to Daphne's. I was very depressed.

Basil came to see me that night. Daphne was still in jail, and very comfortable. She sent me word not to worry, as she was getting new material for speeches, and had two ready.

I refused to see Basil, but he followed the maid back, and stood looking down at me.

"Viv says you saw me," he began without any preamble.

"I did, but I didn't recognise you. You've committed yourself."

He changed colour.

"What else was there to do?" he demanded. "Those two geese would have gone on forever. Viv had the money in his desk, but it was my plan, not his."

As it happened, I had sent father a cablegram about Viv and Poppy just before I was arrested, and now I saw his reply on the mantel.

"Sauce for the goose is sauce for the gander," he had cabled. Well, I had had the jail, and Basil had had—a cold! Basil followed my eyes.

"More cablegrams!" he said. Why doesn't that chap come over and get you?"

"Because I am going back to him. I can't stand the pressure, Basil. Viv and Poppy are all right for this year, but how about next? Is it to be the same thing again?"

"They're going to Italy to live."

"A compromise?" I quoted, rather bitterly. " 'Not

victory but a truce.' You and I made that marriage. It was the T. C. that did it."

Basil took the cablegram from the mantel and deliberately read it. When he got to the signature he drew a long breath and then he grinned.

"So that's that!" he said. "Well, Maggie, are you going back to father, or—staying here with me?"

"You're afraid of me."

"I'll take the risk, Madge. I didn't tell you, Uncle Egbert died while you were away."

"I've been in jail for stealing," I quavered. "And I'd do it again, Basil, for the Cause."

"Bless the Cause," said Basil manfully. "Why shouldn't you vote, if you want to? Aren't you cleverer, and lovelier, and more courageous than any man that ever lived? Anyhow, you're right. Things are rotten. What sane government would lock a man up because his wife refuses to pay her taxes?"

I lifted my head from his shoulder.

"That wretched house at home——" I began.

But he was quite cheerful.

"We'll sell it," he said, "and you shall spend the money for pretties to wear, that don't pay a tax."

It was compromise again. I knew it, but I yielded. After a time I said:

"Basil, what was the retort you gave Poppy about the T. C.?"

"Nothing much," he replied complacently, "I told her, if any one sprung it at her again, to say that if men had made the Ten Commandments, they'd have added an eleventh amendment long ago, or else have annulled them."